THE SHAKESPEARE CONNECTION

Other Oxford Books by Avril Rowlands

Milk and Honey
Poll

The Shakespeare Connection

Avril Rowlands

Oxford University Press
Oxford Toronto Auckland

Oxford University Press, Walton Street, Oxford OX2 6DP

Oxford New York Toronto
Delhi Bombay Calcutta Madras Karachi
Kuala Lumpur Singapore Hong Kong Tokyo
Nairobi Dar es Salaam Cape Town
Melbourne Auckland Madrid

and associated companies in
Berlin Ibadan

Oxford is a trade mark of Oxford University Press

A CIP catalogue record for this book is available
from the British Library

ISBN 0 19 271710 3

Printed and bound in Great Britain by
Biddles Ltd, Guildford and King's Lynn

To my sister Linda
with love and happy memories of the hours we spent
watching Shakespeare's plays at the Old Vic

ACKNOWLEDGEMENTS

Quotations from *A Midsummer Night's Dream*, *Love's Labour's Lost*, *Hamlet*, and *Henry V* are taken from *William Shakespeare: The Complete Works*, General Editors, Stanley Wells and Gary Taylor. Published by Oxford University Press, 1988.

Extracts from *William Shakespeare, A Compact Documentary Life*, by S. Schoenbaum, published by Oxford University Press, 1987, are reprinted by kind permission of Oxford University Press.

I would like to thank the guides and staff at the Shakespeare Birthplace Trust for their help in researching this book and especially Dr Robert Smallwood, Deputy Director and Head of Education, for being kind enough to read the final draft. My grateful thanks are also due to N.W.R. Mellon, Headmaster, King Edward VI School; Prue Dunn of the Royal Shakespeare Theatre; Michael Hampel, and my friend Pattie Taylor, for their assistance. Finally I would like to thank my editor, Marilyn Watts, for her patience and support.

Prologue

The room was quiet, its stillness broken only by the sound of the quill pen as it scratched across the surface of the paper.

'In the year of our Lord, 1596, and in the glorious reign of her Majesty, Queen Elizabeth I, I write this account of the events that have so recently befallen, events that have left their mark on us all . . .'

The pen faltered and stopped as the writer looked up. The window was open and a breeze filled the room, ruffling the parchment sheets on the table. Outside, the garden lay golden in the late-afternoon sun.

Across the grey-stone courtyard and set well back into the shelter of an arbour was a wooden bench. A man dressed in black was sitting there. His face was upturned to catch the last warmth of the sun. His hair receded from his high domed forehead and his eyes were closed.

There was a gust of wind and the man opened his eyes. He turned his head away from the house, as if he expected someone to emerge from the old barn at the end of the garden, now almost hidden in the shadows that were lengthening across the grass. He looked tense and expectant. His hands gripped the sides of the bench. He looked, but no one came, and the man shivered slightly and drew his cloak closer around him.

The quill was dipped into the inkwell and the writing continued, '. . . for it is needful that these things be written down and I will recount them as faithfully as I can.'

The pen hesitated above the parchment and the writer sighed. Now, in the simplicity of the autumn afternoon, as

1

the light slowly began to fade from the room in which she sat, it seemed such a heavy task to have set and one so complicated to unravel. She bent her head to the desk.

'It began with the taking of the manuscript and the appearance of the stranger . . .'

Chapter One

'Go on, go on!' The impatient voice sounded behind the log-jam of people who were trying to squeeze their way through the narrow passage which led to the garden.

'Go on!'

Heads turned as the voice sounded more authoritative, having seen the cause of the trouble. 'Cal, what *are* you doing? Will you stop blocking the doorway please!'

John Loveday pushed his way through the crowd and grasped the tall thin boy firmly by the arm.

'It's always you, isn't it,' he said, half resigned, half exasperated.

Cal shrugged. 'Okay, okay,' he said equably. 'Keep your shirt on.'

They stared at one another for a moment in mutual dislike then John released his grip.

'Can't any of you converse in anything but trite American colloquialisms?' he asked lightly.

'Hey, I guess not,' called a voice from behind.

'We're just a bunch of thickoes,' called another and the kids laughed derisively. John Loveday had not made himself popular with this particular group.

Cal gave a wry smile and another half-shrug then stepped into the garden and breathed in lungfuls of herb-scented air.

He didn't want yet another tussle with Mr Loveday. They always seemed to be fighting. Cal moodily kicked the tiny box hedge that bordered the path. For a moment he even felt sorry for their guide for having to conduct groups of bored kids around and listen to their cynical comments. It must be tough, Cal thought. The moment passed. Mr

3

Loveday was getting paid for it, Cal reflected, and presumably he had wanted the job. Why waste sympathy?

He frowned and kicked the box hedge once more, releasing further scents of lavender and thyme into the air. The elderly Chinese lady who was walking alongside glanced at him in alarm.

The garden smiled in the sunshine, timeless and peaceful, despite the crowds of people in their twentieth-century clothes, cameras slung over their shoulders, guidebooks in their hands; despite the babble of voices in half a dozen different languages.

Something about the garden had stopped Cal in the passage from the Birthplace Trust's modern building. He had hesitated in the doorway, half afraid to cross the threshold. Was it the quality of the light, or was it the half-seen outlines, transparent against the sun's rays, which were there and not there as he looked and looked again? Most probably it was the brushing of something at the back of his neck, no more than a light breath, a touch, a catspaw of fear that had stopped him, causing the crush of people and the anger of Mr Loveday.

The queue to enter the house stretched right into the garden and Cal came to a stop at the tail end. The old house leaned drunkenly before him. The house in which Shakespeare had most probably been born and the home in which he had been brought up. He felt another gentle stirring of the hairs at the base of his neck but this time they only gave rise to a spurt of irritation.

Shakespeare, Cal thought. Okay, so he was the greatest poet and playwright that had ever been, not that Cal had been too impressed when they had done *The Merchant of Venice* in High School. Okay, so the guy had lived around four hundred years ago, and just to have lived that long ago and still have thousands of tourists flocking to your home town must mean something—even, Cal thought cynically, if it only meant a keen nose for business on behalf of the

4

Stratford-upon-Avon Council—OKAY, but why oh why did *he* have to be involved, have to play the tourist, see the sights? Especially now when everything inside him longed to be back home in Worcester, Pennsylvania, USA.

'Try not to look even more bored than I know you are,' said a caustic voice in his ear.

Cal whipped round. 'Quit bugging me, will you!'

John Loveday raised an eyebrow. 'I beg your pardon,' he said with elaborate courtesy and moved to the head of the queue.

Cal felt stifled. The scents of summer, the laughter of his friends, the chattering of the crowds—they seemed to be closing in. Gene glanced at him but Cal pretended not to notice. He turned to get out of the queue, but just then it shuffled forwards and Cal was carried over the threshold into the cool of the low-ceilinged room. A guide from the Birthplace Trust expertly parried the barrage of questions and comments.

'Say, lady, what about the *bathrooms*? What did they do about *bathrooms* for goodness' sake?'

'Please, madam, can you tell me the way out please?'

'Hey, Jasper, it's pretty big, huh? I'd figured he lived in a mud hut. It *is* the original isn't it? You hear that, Jasper? The lady says it's the original.'

'Was he royal—Shakespeare, I mean? Was he connected with royalty?'

'*Signora, per favore . . .*'

'*Ici, mes enfants, attendez-ici!*'

'I prefer stately homes myself, don't you, Mavis? More to look at.'

Cal could stand it no longer. Blindly he turned and fought his way back down the queue.

'Here, lad, you can't go out here. This is the way in . . .'

Cal ignored him and pushed his way out of the door and into the garden.

'Where do you think you're going?'

5

'Sorry. Excuse me. Sorry,' Cal muttered as he shouldered his way back down the narrow path, pushing and jostling the waiting queue. He edged into the passage, crossed the hall, down the steps, and out into the street. There he stopped for a moment, looked around and slowly ambled off.

He wandered aimlessly down Henley Street and into Bridge Street, looking into shop windows with no special interest and staring at the crowds who all seemed—to his resentful eyes—to be happily enjoying themselves. He jay-walked from one side of the road to the other and back again, threading his way through the almost stationary traffic, taking a perverse delight in the black looks and occasional hooting from motorists.

He made his way to the Bancroft Gardens and stopped for a minute to gaze at the brightly-painted narrow-boats moored in the canal. Then he crossed the close-cut lawns and threw himself on to the grassy bank beside the Gower Memorial.

The Memorial was a favourite spot for tourists. Cal watched idly as a portly American gentleman, bald head damp in the sun, wound himself around the statue of Lady Macbeth. The man's wife—a video camera on her shoulder—egged him on.

'Go on, hon, get closer. Give her a big kiss!'

'Like this?' the man asked anxiously.

'That's it, sweetie. Hold it there!'

Excitedly she began shooting, while the man held his precarious position.

Cal was not the only person watching the couple. Standing close to the statue of Falstaff was a young girl.

'You still shooting?' panted the man. 'I can't hold this much longer.'

'I guess so,' said his wife uncertainly.

The man, sweating profusely, slid from Lady Macbeth's arms and collapsed on to the stone plinth at her feet.

6

'Say, do you press the same button to stop the darn thing?'

The video camera was pointing towards Cal. He sat up, stared into the lens and poked out his tongue.

'Well really!' the lady said indignantly, and marched off. The watching girl burst out laughing.

A pleasure boat, filled with excited tourists, passed down the River Avon, leaving a gentle wash and the sound of the amplified commentary.

'If you look on your left, ladies and gentlemen, you will see the Royal Shakespeare Theatre, re-opened in 1932 after the fire in 1926 that demolished its predecessor. Yes, it does look rather like a ship, madam . . .'

The commentary faded as the boat chugged on its way and the ripples left by its passing spread wider and wider. Two swans swam by, stately necks held high. Cal, who had been sitting on the bank staring vacantly into the water, picked up a small stone and aimed it half-heartedly. It fell far short of the swan.

'You shouldn't do that.'

Cal turned round. The girl who had been at the Gower Memorial was standing a few feet away, staring at him resentfully.

'It's cruel.'

'I missed anyway,' Cal was stung into retorting.

'That's not the point. Anyway, they're protected. By the Queen, I think. You can get fined or imprisoned or something if you kill a swan.'

She screwed up her eyes thoughtfully. 'I expect they put you in the Tower of London.'

Cal shrugged and turned back to the river. He did not want to talk to anyone, especially to a know-all kid. But the girl did not take the hint. She came closer and plumped herself on the bank beside him.

'I saw you earlier and thought I'd follow you,' she said. 'I'm practising following people because I'm going to be a detective when I'm older.' She glanced at him anxiously. 'You didn't spot me, did you?'

Cal stared at the river.

'Don't talk much, do you?' the girl said. She paused, but Cal did not respond. 'I saw you making faces at those awful Americans,' she went on. 'I *hate* American tourists, don't you?'

'I'm one,' Cal said shortly.

He glanced at the girl, but she did not seem at all put out. She seemed, if anything, cross with him.

'Well, how was I to know? You don't look like one.' She looked at him, considering. 'They always look sort of squeaky clean. You don't. I thought you were Australian. Or possibly Canadian. I'm usually pretty good at working out who people are.' She stopped. 'Are you *sure* you're American? You're not having me on or anything?'

Cal glanced at her once more. She was younger than him, a scrubby sort of kid in her school uniform. Her once-white shirt hung loose over her short tight black skirt and her tie was half-unknotted. She was short and a little on the plump side, with a round face, freckles, and dark curly hair. She dived enthusiastically into a plastic bag, scattering books around her on the bank.

'Don't you find school books just get heavier and heavier?' she asked, busily sorting and re-packing her bag. 'I'm sure my arms get longer every day. I'll probably end up like a . . . hang on . . .' She hunted for a book, opened it, flicked through the pages, found what she was looking for and carefully read out: ' . . . an Alouatta Beelzebub.' She looked up at Cal. 'Know what that means?'

Cal, despite himself, shook his head.

'It means,' she said triumphantly, referring again to the book. 'It means a howler monkey. The accurate translation is "howling devil". I bet you didn't know that they're the noisiest animals in the world, either.'

She glanced at Cal over the top of the book and Cal shook his head once more.

8

'Well, they are.' She closed the book and stuffed it into her bag. 'I expect I'll end up like one of them. Monkeys need long arms to swing from trees and I'll get long arms because of all these books. Are you here on your own?'

Her abrupt change of topic startled Cal into speaking.

'No.'

'With your parents then?'

Cal got to his feet and began to walk off. The girl scrambled to hers and followed.

'Don't you want to talk?' she called.

Cal did not answer.

'Been told not to talk to strange women have you?' Surprised, Cal paused and stared at her. She was laughing. 'It's all right, I won't attack you, honest.'

She had a nice laugh and her smile lit up her entire face. Cal waited for her to catch up and they walked on together.

'What's your name? Mine's Nicky.'

'Cal.'

'What?'

'That's my name. Cal.'

Nicky tried it out. 'Cal. Cal. Funny name. What's it short for?'

'Calvin. Calvin Hartfield Junior.'

'That's a bit of a mouthful,' said Nicky, impressed.

They walked on in silence.

'How old are you?'

'This an inquest or something?' Cal demanded.

Nicky shrugged. 'Just making polite conversation.'

Cal glanced at her.

'Fourteen. I'm fourteen.'

'Oh.' There was a pause. 'I'm twelve.'

She was only a kid, Cal thought. He wished, irritably, that she would go away.

'That's the weir and Shakespeare's buried in the church behind,' she said, pointing helpfully at the far bank.

Cal pulled a face. 'You sound like Loveday.'

9

'Who?' She sounded startled.

'Loveday. Our guide. He keeps spouting that sort of stuff. We call him "The Stiff". You know, dead from the feet up.'

Nicky looked uncomprehending.

'He's a real Brit,' Cal explained. 'Stiff upper lip and all that.'

Nicky fired up. 'You've got a funny idea of us, haven't you?'

'Hey?'

'You Americans. You don't know what we're like at all. I bet you think we all live in olde-worlde cottages with roses round the door and that we touch our forelocks—whatever they are—to the squire. You do, don't you? And I bet you think the squire's terribly, terribly British—huntin', shootin', and fishin'. That's what you think, isn't it?'

'I don't know,' Cal said in an injured voice, angry at the attack on him. 'I never thought about it.'

'You tourists make me sick,' Nicky said vehemently. 'Uuggh!' She pretended to be sick into the river.

'Hey, let's get this straight,' Cal said hotly. 'I couldn't care less about Shakespeare, Stratford, or the Brits in general. I never even thought about it until I had to come on this God-awful tour. So quit it, right?'

He walked on in angry silence.

'Aren't you interested in Shakespeare?' Nicky asked in a different tone of voice.

'Nope.'

'I thought all Americans were. I'm not, but then I live here so it's different. I know it all anyway,' she finished airily. 'Why did you come?'

'School trip.'

'Oh.' She glanced at him. 'You don't sound as if you're enjoying it.'

Cal shrugged his shoulders and they walked on in silence.

* * *

'Are we meant to be gratified at the return of the wanderer?' was John Loveday's sour comment, when Cal eventually returned to the guest house where his group was staying.

Cal ignored him. 'Hi, you guys,' he said to the assembled company.

Most of the occupants of the lounge had their eyes firmly fixed on the television. Lou was reading, while Carole was contorted in aerobic exercises.

John followed Cal into the room and raised his voice. 'If I might just have your attention for a moment . . .'

The television watchers reluctantly looked up at him.

'Turn it off, Greg, you've got the remote.'

'Okay, okay.'

John sat on the arm of a chair. 'The itinerary for tomorrow. In the morning we go to Anne Hathaway's cottage, which is a mile away at Shottery. Anne Hathaway, as I'm sure you know, was Shakespeare's wife. They were married in 1582. He was then 18 years old and Anne was 26 . . .'

'Say, wasn't she a bit old for him?' asked Carole, from an upside-down position on the floor.

'Perhaps he was her toy boy,' sniggered Gene.

'He got her pregnant and in those days they had to get married,' said Lou, who prided herself on her knowledge of Shakespeare.

'Is that so?' said Greg, admiringly. He rather fancied Lou.

John cut in sharply. 'Then we go on to Mary Arden's house at Wilmcote—Mary Arden was Shakespeare's mother, as I'm sure Lou could tell us—and after that we go to Hall's Croft—where his daughter, Susanna, lived with her husband John Hall, an eminent doctor. We end the day at New Place, where Shakespeare lived in later years. You are free in the evening—heaven help the inhabitants of

11

Stratford! Wednesday morning we tour backstage at the Royal Shakespeare Theatre and in the afternoon we travel to London. The coach will be here tomorrow at nine o'clock sharp and I mean sharp. I'll expect all of you to be ready—and I mean *all* of you—Cal included. Goodnight.'

As he rose from the chair Greg was already aiming the remote control at the television set. John stopped in the doorway.

'Cal. I want a word with you.'

Cal followed him out of the room.

'We missed your entertaining company this afternoon,' said John sarcastically. 'I imagine you had a pressing prior engagement?'

Cal said nothing.

'No? Or perhaps you felt, like Lou, that you knew it all?'

Cal stared at the wall opposite, his face a mask of indifference.

'However,' John continued icily. 'However, you are— unfortunately for us both—in my charge during this trip. You are my responsibility. It was—to put it mildly— extremely discourteous of you to leave the group without permission, explanation, or apology. You will not do it again. Do I make myself clear?'

There was a long silence.

'Yessir,' Cal muttered at last.

John crossed the hall to the doorway. 'Your parents paid a lot of money for you to come on this trip,' he said. 'You don't want to let them down, do you?'

With that he went.

'Yeah,' said Cal bitterly, speaking to the empty hall. 'They paid a whole heap of money. Anything to get me out of the way.'

Chapter Two

Cal tossed and turned, unable to sleep. He wished he had the nerve to get up and go out, but he shied away from the complications—how to dress in the dark for instance, and how not to wake his room mates if he turned on the light. Then there was the difficulty of getting out of the guest house and the greater difficulty of returning unnoticed. Weak, that's what I am, he thought bitterly.

He sat up in bed and looked at the luminous figures on his watch. Two o'clock. Hours to go before it was time to get up. Hours before breakfast. He was suddenly ravenously hungry and remembered that he had had no supper, other than an ice-cream and a bag of crisps. He thought of the ice-cream and tortured himself with the memory of its fresh minty taste. The kid—what was her name?—had had strawberry, and insisted on paying for her own. What *was* her name? Nicky—that was it. He was half sorry now that he had not asked for her surname or taken her address or made any plan to see her.

Boy, was he hungry. He felt on his bedside table and found the remains of a bar of chocolate.

'Eureka,' he said quietly. He lay back in bed eating it slowly, making every piece last. Not much point in making any plans, he thought, we won't be here that long. Day after tomorrow it's London. He munched thoughtfully at his chocolate and listened to the slight noises around him: the quiet breathing of Gene and Franklin; the odd creak of a floorboard; the distant traffic.

Soon we'll be going home. Home. It had a nice sound, a comforting sound. He finished the chocolate and screwed the wrapper into a ball. Home. That was a joke. A picture of his mother's face came into his mind, round and soft and anxious, her eyes full of worry.

He could hear her voice, gentle, cajoling, filled with maternal concern. 'But, Cal honey, it's such an opportunity. You can't throw it over.'

He could hear his own voice, trying to sound calm. 'But I don't want to go.'

His mother placed a protective arm around his shoulders. 'But it's better for you to be out of this. Things could get real nasty. You're too young to be mixed up.'

'I'm not. I'm not too young.'

'Sure you are.'

Cal remembered the silence that had fallen between them, while he struggled not to say the words that he knew would be better left unsaid.

'Can't I see him?' The words burst out. He had to continue then, trying not to let his voice crack, trying not to show how much he cared, trying, above all, not to plead. 'Perhaps if I saw him, I could sort something out between you . . .'

His mother was shocked. 'Your father? See your father? Are you mad?'

'I—I just thought . . .'

'Over my dead body,' she snapped, her usually gentle voice cold and hard. She looked at Cal and softened. 'Come on, Cal-boy, your momma's under a lot of pressure right now. I'm fighting this for you, not for me. So you go on that trip, huh?' She pressed her soft cheek to his and Cal, his stomach churning as much from the smell of her heavy scent as from the situation, had cravenly given in.

Cal lay rigid in bed and anger at himself burned deep. He had given in, lamely, weakly, without a fight, because it was easier that way. Just like his father had always given in to his mother, time after time after time, until the day something had snapped and he had walked out for good.

14

He screwed his eyes up tight, but a tear forced its way through the shut lids and down his cheek. He would not cry. Dammit, he *would not*! He turned over and pummelled the pillows hard with his fists.

'Cut it out, can't you?' came a drowsy voice from the next bed.

Cal pulled the duvet over his head and willed himself to sleep.

'Burgers are on Cal tonight,' said Gene decisively.

'Hey, why me?' Cal asked.

'One. You kept us awake half the night fighting with the bedclothes. What did you have in there with you—an elephant? Two. You made "The Stiff" even madder than usual when you said you were going to pass out in the garden of that old house we were in—where was it, Lou?'

'New Place,' Lou said crisply.

'Yeah. That's it. I remember. Say, why do they call a house as old as that "New"?'

Lou sighed. 'Because it was new when Shakespeare bought it. At least,' she continued, a stickler for the truth, 'the house we saw wasn't the original one Shakespeare lived in. That got pulled down and only the foundations are left. We walked round them, remember? It was there that Cal went funny.'

'Is that so?' said Gene, not understanding a word. He turned his attention back to Cal. 'Anyway, if you turned funny for some kind of a joke, you might have let us know beforehand and we'd have ducked the riot act. Boy, was he angry,' he said appreciatively, 'I couldn't understand half the words he used and I bet you couldn't either, Lou.'

'It wasn't a joke,' Cal said.

'In that case you should see a medic. Just leave us your money, go back to the guest house and Mrs Walters will be delighted to put you to bed and ring for the doc.' He regarded Cal thoughtfully. 'And three, if you want a three.

15

I'm bushed and I'm broke. Double cheeseburger, double fries, and a large Coke might, just might, revive me. What about you guys?'

'I'm bushed, too,' Cal retorted.

'But not broke, sweetie,' said Carole, who had taken off her trainers and socks and was busy massaging her feet.

Franklin wrinkled his nose. 'Wowee! Easy way to empty the restaurant.'

'Oh, put a sock in it,' said Carole and threw one of hers in his face. He fielded it neatly.

'I didn't know you cared so much,' he said, tying it round his neck. 'It'll cost you some to get it back.'

'Okay, what'll you all have?' asked Cal, resignedly.

The group were lounging at a table in the window of McDonald's Restaurant in Bridge Street. It had been a long, hot day and everyone was tired, bad-tempered, and hungry. Cal took the orders and joined the queue for food. When he returned to his seat with the stacked-up cardboard containers, Gene grabbed the topmost Coke and took a long drink.

'Boy, I needed that!' he said appreciatively.

Carole stretched, cat-like, in her seat. 'If I never go round another Elizabethan house for the rest of my life, I won't complain,' she said. 'Anyone fancy a bathe later on? They've got a swell pool here.'

Greg turned to Lou. 'Is there such a thing as cultural indigestion? If so, I've got it.'

'Why does everyone ask me these things?' Lou complained.

'Because you're the smart-ass,' he replied.

'Thanks a bunch,' Lou replied, half-offended, half-pleased.

Cal passed round the food, then sank into his seat. Gee, I'm tired, he thought. He nibbled a french fry and looked at the faces around him. He felt oddly removed, as if he were a stranger who just happened to be sitting at the same

16

table. None of them were close friends, anyway, they were just class-mates thrown together on this one occasion.

There was Gene, tall and broad-shouldered, good at football. He thought himself the leader of the group. Then there was Greg, sandy-haired and sharp-faced, who was letting his food go cold as he gazed longingly at Lou. Franklin, munching his way through a double helping of french fries; Carole, the keep-fit fanatic who went jogging every morning . . . and the rest of the group who had decided to go for a pizza rather than a hamburger. Cal felt uninvolved with them, distant . . .

He picked up his hamburger and looked out of the window. It was still light and the street was crowded with people, many of them heading purposefully towards the river. Probably going to the theatre, Cal thought. He glanced at his watch. Seven-fifteen.

'What time's the theatre start?' he asked.

He took a bite of hamburger, and a trickle of tomato ketchup ran down his chin. Should have asked for a burger without ketchup, he thought. He'd never liked the stuff.

Nicky—wasn't that Nicky out there?

Quickly he looked away. She couldn't have seen him, could she? He felt embarrassed and exposed in his window seat. He wished he could move, do something.

'Any of you guys want another Coke?' he asked.

No one answered. He glanced out of the window again, a furtive glance. It *was* her, standing on the pavement, staring straight at him, her face unusually solemn. Cal turned away. He'd be the laughing stock of the group if they thought a little English kid was chasing him. It was all he needed.

He raised his hamburger to take another bite. He was suddenly hot, too hot. His clothes were sticking to him, his hair clinging to his scalp, beads of sweat running into his eyes. Perhaps I *am* sick, he thought. Perhaps I do need a medic. Lou was looking at him and saying something but

17

he could not hear what it was. There was a noise in his ears, like a rushing of water. His chest felt tight and he could not breathe. He turned again to the window. She was still there, the girl. It was not Nicky, it was nothing like Nicky, but she was willing him outside, he had to go, he had to get out of the restaurant . . . into some air . . .

He stood up with an effort, the hamburger still in his hand. He must have made some excuse, although he was sure he did not speak, because no one seemed bothered by his going. He felt grateful for that. He went to the door, opened it, and stepped outside. A draught of fresh air blew into his face and he took a deep breath.

Oh boy, that was better!

He took another deep breath, then another, filling his lungs. The feeling of panic subsided, leaving him weak and shaky. He leaned against the door jamb, eyes half-closed, and stared vacantly across the street.

Funny, he thought idly, the way those buildings opposite are disappearing. Looks kind of odd . . . the Mulberry Tree Shopping Centre, Marks and Spencer, those gift shops . . . they look so thin . . . transparent almost . . . He shifted his gaze to the road, to the slowly-moving traffic and the cars parked solidly on either side . . . nothing solid about them now, he thought, he could see right through them . . .

A Midland Red bus stopped outside the restaurant and cut off Cal's view. He watched the bustle as people got on and off, then it drew away from the kerb. Wonder if that'll fade too, Cal thought, vaguely interested. Yep, there it goes, just an outline . . . He watched its progress up the street. Crazy, the way you can see those people sitting inside the bus. They're sitting inside nothing . . . and on nothing . . . and they've become nothing . . .

The passengers on the bus, the crowds thronging the pavements, everyone slowly growing thin and insubstantial . . . outlines, forms without substance . . . then the outlines faded . . . and over all was silence, total silence . . .

18

At least, Cal thought, that noise in my head has stopped.

The full force of what was happening hit him in a sudden wave of shock, so violent that it felt like a physical blow. The street, as he knew it, had almost gone. Thin outlines hung in the air, like the remains of a pencilled sketch imperfectly rubbed out, still to be seen under the fresh drawing that was replacing it, even as he watched.

He turned to the top of the street. The roundabout had vanished; so too, had the building beyond, which housed Barclays Bank. The pedestrian crossing was dissolving.

Then the light of the sun was cut off. As Cal watched, a row of houses superimposed themselves along the central reservation of the wide street. The buildings quickly gained substance with colour and texture—wooden-beamed houses with rough plaster in between, their upper stories jutting out over the lower. Some, Cal could see, were dwellings, while others were shops, their doors invitingly open and their wares displayed on wooden shelves hung beneath small-paned windows. An avenue of trees sprang up in front of the buildings, their bare branches quickly clothed with dark green leaves.

Cal blinked. Under the trees were people, some strolling, others walking purposefully, some standing gossiping. The women wore long dresses. The men . . .

'. . . Elizabethan gentlemen wore breeches, doublet, and hose. They carried small knives with which to cut up their food and many of them wore swords . . .'

Cal shook his head sharply. Where had he heard those words? They came into his mind ready formed, as if a voice was speaking inside his head, a curt, impatient voice speaking clearly in the silence that surrounded him. He thought for a moment. Of course, it had been their guide, Mr Loveday. He had said those words, or something like them, when he had shown the group round the exhibition of costumes from Shakespeare's plays.

The street was quickly filling up. Old men sat in doorways, children ran to and fro, housewives bartered for goods, young men swaggered past. A woman moved from person to person with a tray containing a jumble of ribbons, handkerchiefs, pins, and brooches slung round her neck. The tray rested against her large stomach and wobbled each time she opened her mouth to shout her wares. A young blind boy sat under a tree playing on a reed pipe. Three dogs burst out of an alleyway, fighting savagely, and a flock of sheep caused havoc as they were herded up the street by a purposeful shepherd-boy. The street was alive, but silent. Quite silent.

A cart made a slow and noiseless progress through the crowds. Dust rose in spirals as the wheels bit into the hard-packed soil which formed the surface of the road. Cal watched the dust cloud rise into the air and hang over the houses.

The driver cracked his whip and the sound cut through the silence like a knife and dispersed it. Cal reeled as the noise hit him, wave upon wave, a symphony of voices, shouts and cries, while over all, clear and plaintive, came the thin reed sound of a pipe.

With the sounds came the smells which were full-blooded and over-ripe. The mixture of odours made Cal retch. One smell dominated: the succulence of cooked meat, hot and sizzling in its own gravy.

But it was not the sounds or the smells that brought Cal fully to his senses. It was the pain in his hand. The hamburger he held was hot and burning his fingers. He glanced down.

He was no longer holding a hamburger, wrapped in a paper napkin. Instead, held in a very grubby hand, was a meat pie, and boiling gravy was oozing out of the one bite that had been taken. He dropped the pie to the ground and licked his burnt fingers.

'Goddammit!' he swore.

'Oh pray do not swear, sir!'

A girl was standing a few feet away, staring at him with a mixture of curiosity and resentment. Cal stared back. She had light-brown hair brushed away from a protruding forehead, a plain, rather sallow face, a long nose and wide green eyes.

Cal passed an unsteady hand across his face and tried to think. Drugs, he wondered? Did one of the kids lace his hamburger? Or was it some monstrous practical joke? The girl watched him, her gaze unwavering and somehow disconcerting. He felt that he was being judged.

'Is this some kind of a joke?' he demanded.

'Joke?' the girl repeated.

One of the fighting dogs made a sudden snap at the pie and Cal jumped. The dog seized it and ran off, its rivals hard on its heels.

'Come,' said the girl impatiently, 'we are already late.'

She gathered up her long skirt and began to walk swiftly up the street.

Cal ran after her. 'Hey, wait a minute,' he called. 'Wait!'

The girl stopped and turned.

'I want some answers to some questions . . .' Cal began.

'I can tell you nothing,' the girl said curtly. 'It was not my idea to meet you.'

She started walking again and Cal followed more slowly, looking round him with some curiosity. A thought struck. 'Hey!' he called after her. 'Hey, is this a film set?'

The girl stopped again and wrinkled her forehead. 'Film? I don't understand . . .'

'But . . .'

The girl was already walking on, more slowly this time, pushing her way through the crowds. They were thicker now, milling at the crossroads at the top of the street and centred around a building which was suspended above the ground on wooden pillars. Tradesmen had spread their goods in its shelter and Cal saw stalls selling fruit, butter, eggs, and cheeses. Chickens ran under people's feet, easily evading a boy with a stick who was trying to catch them; dogs fought, cats were everywhere, and a boy with a vacant expression on his face sat at the foot of a great wooden post which was inset with iron rings, his arm around the neck of a goose.

Directly in front of Cal was a cart containing blocks of salt. A large man stood beside it, his shirt open to the waist, his sleeves rolled up over beefy arms.

'Salt! Salt for sale! Salt!' he shouted, his voice clear above the tumult of talking, shouting, laughing, and cursing.

'What's going on round here?'

'Market day,' the girl said indifferently, but she, too, had stopped.

'My grandfather is there,' she said, nodding towards the covered area under the house. 'He is a glove-maker.' Her voice had softened and Cal, glancing at her, saw her expression soften too. The change was momentary.

'Will you come, please,' she said, impatient once more, and she took his arm.

Cal started, for her hand was warm and firm. More than anything, her touch told him that this was real. He was not in a dream.

He glanced down, shrugging himself free. He saw his arm, no longer clad in a grubby white sweat-shirt. With a sick feeling he saw himself dressed in a dark-blue, tightly-fitting jacket, the sleeves slightly puffed at the shoulders. His comfortable jeans with the hole in the left knee had become much-mended dark-blue breeches and his legs were encased in thick brown tights which were wrinkled round the ankles. Light leather shoes were on his feet. A cold trickle of fear ran down his back.

'I'm not going one step further until you do some explaining,' he said stubbornly.

'I am only a messenger,' the girl said sullenly.

22

Cal said nothing.

'Indeed, my sister will explain,' she continued. 'She was not able to leave the house.'

She turned to walk on, but Cal remained where he was. The girl sighed again.

'It was not my idea to fetch you, but they insisted,' she said. 'I am nobody. I told you.' Her voice was bitter and her face resentful. 'I just do as I am bid.' She looked at Cal with dislike. 'Now, will you come?'

'Who are you?' Cal demanded.

The girl shrugged indifferently. 'My name is Judith,' she said. 'Judith Shakespeare.'

Chapter Three

They left the crossroads and entered a side street. The crowds began to thin and the sounds of the market grew distant. Judith touched Cal's arm and gestured towards a house on the right. He followed her in through a low doorway, ducking his head as he entered.

It was cool inside and dark, so dark that he blundered into a piece of furniture. A hand reached out and grasped his arm and Judith's voice said abruptly, 'Not *that* way.'

She guided him across the room and out through another door. It led directly into a garden. The air was filled with a heavy scent and Cal sniffed. Lavender and thyme. He had an unexpectedly sharp memory of a Chinese lady and a low box hedge. I know this place, he thought suddenly, and then he saw a girl standing on the lawn beside a laurel bush.

She was a slim girl with dark hair brushed smooth on either side of a centre parting. Her expression was composed as she carefully removed the white sheet from the bush over which it had been draped. She pressed it to her cheek before folding it carefully and placing it in a wicker basket that lay at her feet. She caught sight of Cal and straightened.

'This is he?' she asked, almost doubtfully.

'I do not know,' Judith said. 'I just did what you bade.'

'Of course.' She looked at Cal and dropped a slight curtsy.

'Thank you for coming, Master . . . ?'

Cal was confused. 'I beg your pardon?'

'Your name, sir. May we know it?'

'Oh, I see. Cal. That's my name.'

'Cal,' she repeated, as if committing it to memory. 'Cal. I am Susanna, but of course you know that already.'

'No, ma'am,' Cal replied, tongue-tied in front of this calm and self-possessed girl.

'No?' she seemed surprised. 'Judith, run and find Hamnet.'

'I do not know where he is,' Judith said sullenly.

There was a stirring in the branches of the tree above their heads and a boy dropped to the ground. He made a small, neat bow.

'Master Cal, is it not?'

'You've been eavesdropping again,' Judith said accusingly.

'More than that,' the boy said proudly. 'I followed you through town and you never even knew I was there!'

Judith flushed. 'I do not like being spied upon,' she said angrily. The boy laughed and Cal looked from one to the other.

Their voices were the same. They were both of the same height and their features were alike, except that, unlike Judith's, the boy's face was bright and alive with mischief. His eyes danced, while hers were still and catlike. His mouth, too, was fuller and creased into a smile.

'Hamnet, Judith, you forget yourselves in front of our guest!'

Susanna's voice brought both pairs of green eyes back to Cal and he shifted uncomfortably from one foot to the other.

'There is serious business to talk over, Hamnet, or have you forgot so soon?'

Hamnet's bright expression faded.

'Come, take Master Cal to our meeting place,' said Susanna. 'Judith, help me with this washing and we will join you as soon as we may.'

She picked up one end of the heavy basket and Judith, still gazing at Cal, took the other. Their heavy skirts made a

25

swishing sound over the flagstones as they disappeared into the house. Hamnet and Cal were left staring at one another.

'Forgive me for jesting. I did not follow you in town. It was only . . .' Hamnet grinned. 'Judith rises so easily to bait that it is hard not to tease her. Shall we go?' With a courteous wave of his hand he led the way across the grass towards a barn at the far end of the garden.

'We're twins you know,' Hamnet went on, chatting easily. 'Which accounts for us looking so alike although we are not at all alike in temperament. Do you like to fish?' he asked suddenly.

'Why . . .' Cal replied, confused. 'I . . .'

'I love fishing,' Hamnet said enthusiastically. 'I also like fighting and hunting but fishing is best. I like all sports. I like everything in fact,' he added expansively, 'except reading and writing and Latin.' He pulled a face. 'Fulke and I played truant from school the other week. We went to see the bear-baiting. But we met grandfather and he marched us back. We both got beaten. Twice. Once by grandfather and once by the Master. I don't know which of them struck hardest.'

'I'm sorry,' Cal said, after a pause.

'It mattered not,' Hamnet said airily. 'I'm always being beaten for something or other. Even father . . .' he stopped abruptly and his face clouded. 'Even father sometimes beats me, but not often,' he continued more slowly.

He glanced at Cal, the bright look back again. 'You know,' he said confidingly, 'it is good having you to talk to. There are a great many women in this house. Father is away a good deal and grandfather is busy all the time—besides he's old. How old are you?'

'Fourteen,' said Cal.

Hamnet looked surprised. 'That's quite old,' he said. 'Susanna is thirteen and Judith and I are eleven.'

They reached the barn and Hamnet swung himself up on to a branch of an apple tree that grew beside it. 'Let's hide until the girls arrive.'

It was too late. Susanna and Judith were already hurrying across the grass to meet them. They sat down and at once the occasion took on a solemn air.

'So, Master Cal,' Susanna began gravely. 'You say you do not know our story.'

Cal shook his head.

'It is your tale, Hamnet,' Susanna said. 'But make it brief, or mother will come searching for us.'

There was a moment's silence.

'It was my fault, in a way,' Hamnet said at last. He sounded subdued. 'I should never have left father's manuscript, but I was sure I saw a pike and I was only gone for a second or two . . .'

'Begin at the *beginning*,' Judith interrupted. 'Not half-way through.'

'All right.' Hamnet paused to collect his thoughts. 'Father is a player, an actor with the Lord Chamberlain's Men. You must have heard of them, they are famous. He is their main poet as well. They are very good players,' he said enthusiastically, warming to his theme. 'We saw them when they came to Stratford last year. And father writes very good plays. They acted *Romeo and Juliet*, which father wrote. He only had a small part in it but we clapped and cheered when he came on to the stage . . .'

'Hamnet,' said Susanna warningly.

'Yes. Well. I'm sorry. He gave me a new play, one he has just finished writing, and asked me to read it.'

'Father always gives his plays to Hamnet,' Judith said sourly. 'I cannot think why. Hamnet doesn't know good verse from bad.'

'Neither do you,' Hamnet returned hotly. 'You cannot even read!'

Judith said nothing. Cal glanced at her and saw her mouth set in a firm thin line.

'I took it to the riverside and began to read,' Hamnet continued. 'But it's very difficult reading a manuscript. It's

27

different seeing a play on the stage, but reading it is hard.'

He was silent for a moment. 'The sun was shining on the river and I caught sight of a shadow. I was sure it was a pike, there's been a big one which Fulke and I have been trying to catch for some time. So I put the manuscript down and climbed down the bank. No one was around. It's slippery just there and the bank can give way under your feet. You need both hands and you have to concentrate, for the current is swift-flowing. I slipped once but caught hold of a tree stump. I leant over to see the shadow and it *was* the pike, but it swam away as soon as it sensed I was there. Then I climbed back up the bank.'

He stopped and looked down.

'The manuscript had gone,' he finished flatly.

There was silence.

'Perhaps it blew away,' Cal suggested.

'It was a still day,' Hamnet said. 'I searched all round but could not find it. And I had placed a stone on top of the sheets for safe-keeping.'

There was another silence and a feeling of tension. Susanna, Hamnet, and Judith were staring at Cal— Hamnet half-defiant, half-ashamed, Susanna questioning, Judith . . . an odd look. The silence became uncomfortable.

'It'll turn up,' Cal said at last, trying to lighten the atmosphere. 'These things usually do.'

'But this has not,' said Susanna gently. 'Four days have passed since it happened and we have scoured the riverbank and searched the house. The manuscript has gone.'

'Perhaps someone took it . . .'

'That is what we think.'

'And they'll return it when they realize their mistake.'

Again the feeling of tension.

'But by whom? And why?'

Hamnet stirred. 'My sister thinks it was stolen.'

28

Cal looked from one to the other. 'That's crazy. Who'd want to steal it?'

'Another company of players perhaps,' Hamnet answered.

'Why? Surely there's another copy? These things aren't that precious are they?'

Susanna gave him a startled look. 'I see that you do not understand, Master Cal. Perhaps where you come from things are different, but here there is only one or maybe two copies taken. These plays are assets of the company and jealously guarded. Even the players only receive their own parts and not the whole play. And my father has made many enemies by virtue of his success.'

'But that's crazy,' Cal repeated. 'Your father's plays can be bought anywhere, by anyone. You go to any bookshop and you see them on sale. Why I guess they've been translated into most languages in the world.'

There was a long, long silence.

'Where have you come from, stranger?' Susanna asked at last.

'Me? I don't know . . . I guess . . .' Cal found that he was trembling. He looked at the grass on which he sat. It looked so real. He ran his hand over the bright green blades and they felt real, they tickled his palm. He spread out his fingers. It was *his* hand, *his* fingers. He picked up a twig. The wood felt rough to his touch. He bent it and it snapped into two pieces. The noise it made was real and the two halves of the twig lay in front of him.

'I guess I was in Stratford-upon-Avon, England on a tour. But my home is back in Worcester, USA.'

'Worcester?' Hamnet said quickly, eagerly. 'But that's more than a day's journey from here—father took me once.'

'Not that Worcester,' Cal said. 'The one in America. In the United States.'

Three pairs of eyes regarded him steadily.

29

'Look,' Cal said desperately. 'I guess—if this isn't some kind of a joke you guys are playing and if I'm not sick or something . . .' he stared around him, half-expecting Greg and Franklin to emerge from behind a tree in a dark corner of the garden . . .

Nothing, except the sudden sweet sound of a bird.

'Am I right,' Cal went on, choosing his words with care, 'in thinking that your father is William Shakespeare?'

'Of course he is,' said Hamnet proudly.

'You know that already,' Judith said coldly.

'Hush,' said Susanna, her eyes still on Cal.

'What year is it?' Cal asked fearfully.

'The year of our Lord, 1596,' Judith replied promptly.

'Then,' Cal said slowly, his mouth suddenly dry. 'Then I guess you could say I come from four hundred years in the future.'

'But that's impossible!' Judith said vehemently.

'Not impossible, only strange,' Susanna contradicted.

'I think he's some friend, kinsman maybe, of Goody Bromley,' Judith said heatedly. 'Between them they planned this charade, after you went to see her.'

'Why should they do that?'

'To make a May-game of us—to make profit from us—to have power over us.' Judith shivered. 'She is a witch.'

She got up from the grass and walked over to Cal. 'Confess,' she said. 'Confess that you and Goody Bromley are in league.'

'I don't know what you're talking about,' Cal said helplessly.

'You're some poor kinsman of hers from another part of the country.' She turned to the others. 'Can't you hear his strange speech?' She turned back to Cal. 'What did she bribe you with—gold maybe?'

Cal got to his feet. 'You're crazy!' he exclaimed. 'Nobody's bribed me with anything! You can't imagine I wanted this to happen?'

30

'All right then.' Judith stared into Cal's eyes, her own gleaming green. 'If you *are* who you say you are and you *have* come here from the future, then you must have come from the devil. Everyone knows Goody Bromley is a witch.'

'She is not,' Susanna said adamantly. 'She is a wise woman, that's all.'

'Something more than that if she can conjure this creature out of the air.'

'I didn't come out of the air,' Cal protested, understanding only a small part of their meaning. 'I came out of McDonald's Restaurant. And anyway, it was you who beckoned me. I don't know any Goody Bromley or whatever her name is.'

He felt a sharp stinging sensation and gave a sudden cry. He looked in disbelief at the cut in his wrist and the blood that was beginning to ooze out.

'That settles it,' said Hamnet. His face was white and his voice shook slightly as he sheathed a small, sharp knife. 'He cannot be from the devil if he can feel pain. The devil cannot feel pain.'

'You cut me with that?' Cal asked, incredulously. 'You're crazy, all of you!' He began to suck his wrist.

'It was a test,' Hamnet said seriously. He looked at the blood on Cal's fingers. 'I don't think that the devil sheds blood either,' he added doubtfully. 'But I'm not sure.'

He suddenly held his dagger up by the point, so that the hilt, forming a cross, was in front of Cal's eyes. It gleamed silver in a shaft of sunlight.

'You see?' Hamnet said. 'He did not cover his eyes nor turn his head when confronted by the cross of Christ. No devil can withstand the true cross.'

'Brother, have done,' said Susanna. 'Do not jest about these things. They are serious matters.'

'I do not jest,' Hamnet replied, offended. 'I, too, take them seriously, therefore I have tested the stranger and found that he has not come from the devil.'

31

Judith snorted. 'The devil comes in many guises,' she said darkly. 'I still think him kin to Goody Bromley.'

'Well, I think him true,' said Susanna gravely, 'and I think he speaks truth. He is sent in answer to a prayer. Sit down, Judith, Hamnet,' she went on with quiet authority. 'I think you both owe Master Cal an apology.'

'That's okay,' Cal mumbled. He sat down on the bank.

'I, at least, owe you an explanation,' Susanna went on. 'When we failed to find the manuscript, it was my idea to go to Mistress Bromley. She is a wise woman with many gifts of healing and is skilled in finding that which is lost.'

'She also makes love potions,' Judith put in unexpectedly.

'I was afraid,' Susanna said seriously, 'for I do not know whether it is right to dabble in—not witchcraft—but magic of a sort. Perhaps I did wrong, but it was my decision to go and I can do no other than stand by it.'

She was silent for a moment. It was very still in the garden and the evening shadows were beginning to lengthen across the lawn.

'I went to her cottage, knocked on the door and entered. She seemed to be expecting me. She did not even look up as I went inside. "You seek something that is missing," she said straight away. "Come closer, child." I went closer and she sat me down on a stool at her feet. She took the poker and thrust it into the fire. Sparks flew up and stuck to the soot on the chimney where they remained, glowing brightly. She stared at them for a long time as if reading something in the patterns they made. Still she did not speak and it grew late. I must have made some movement for she put out her hand to me. Then she said . . .' Susanna paused, trying to recall the exact words. 'She said, "I see sorrow and pain for you and your family. You will know the bitterness of parting. But restoration of a kind will happen, one with another." I did not and do not understand what she meant by that. But when I tried to ask her she held my hand more tightly and said, "I see a stranger from a strange land. He will come to aid you." She told me where and when I was to meet you, she even told me what you would be wearing.' Susanna stopped.

Cal was silent.

'So what am I meant to do?' he asked at last.

'That she did not say,' Susanna admitted.

Hamnet stirred impatiently. 'It's obvious. You must find the manuscript.'

There was another silence.

'Hey, wait a minute,' Cal said slowly. 'There's something here I just don't get.' He turned to Hamnet. 'Your father gave you his new play to read, right?'

Hamnet nodded.

'And it disappeared while you were fishing, right?'

Hamnet nodded again.

'Okay. Don't you see, it's simple? How come your father didn't stroll by and take his play back, seeing you didn't want to know?'

Hamnet looked confused. 'I don't understand.'

'Okay. So your father might have been walking past, on the riverbank. He might have seen that you were more interested in fishing than in reading his new masterpiece and taken it back. How's that sound?'

'No,' said Susanna. 'Father went to Leicester with the Company. He was away when it happened. He is now back in London.'

'Have you told him what's happened?'

'No,' said Hamnet loudly.

'Why not?'

'He was only home for a short time. I could not . . .' Hamnet's face was bright red.

'He'd beat him and it would do him good,' Judith said caustically.

Hamnet turned on her. 'You think I care for a beating?' he demanded hotly.

33

'Father would be hurt,' Susanna said. 'He would regard it with great sadness that Hamnet, who was entrusted with the work, set so little store by it that he left it in order to play.'

'I wasn't playing, I was fishing!' Hamnet protested. 'And I don't set little store by it. I just—just found it difficult.'

There was a pause.

'You must understand, Master Cal, that Hamnet is thoroughly spoilt,' Judith said drily. 'He is the apple of father's eye, the son and heir. He cannot afford to let father know that he is less than perfect.'

'Judith, that's unfair!' Susanna said sharply. 'Of course father would be hurt. 'Tis not right to burden him with this.' She turned to Cal. 'He has many cares and is a busy man.'

'But if you told him, you might find he has another copy,' Cal urged.

'There was only one,' Hamnet said miserably. 'He told me it was the first draft of *Love's Labour's Won* and that I must take care of it.'

'*Love's Labour's Won?*' Cal said eagerly. 'I think I've heard of it. I'm *sure* I have—or something like it. I'll check it out when I get back.' He stopped suddenly as full realization swept over him. '*If* I get back,' he amended miserably.

He looked round. It was growing dark and the corner of the garden in which they sat was darker still. He could just make out the figures sitting opposite—Hamnet on the branch of the tree, moodily playing with his knife, Susanna seated on a low hump of grass, her sister a little to one side, her face in shadow. All he could really see of Judith was the white ruff around her neck and the lighter blur of her face . . .

'So where do I come into the picture?' Cal heard himself saying.

'I don't know . . .'

' . . . know . . . know . . . know . . .'

34

It was Susanna's voice, but the echo came from elsewhere. The apple tree looked strange . . . it was bearing down on him, its branches waving like arms . . . Cal felt sick and dizzy. He concentrated on the ruff around Judith's neck, only it was not a ruff at all but a sock, a white sock and it was not around Judith's neck but draped, inelegantly, around Franklin's.

Franklin's voice came, as if from a great distance, 'I don't know . . .'

And Cal found himself sitting in McDonald's Restaurant, his mouth full of hamburger and bun.

'Don't know what?' he mumbled, confused.

'What time the theatre starts,' Franklin replied. 'Though I don't know why *you* want to know. Not thinking of going are you?'

'What?'

'Say, you okay?' Lou asked suddenly. 'You look awful.'

Cal glanced, half-fearfully, at his reflection in the window. He saw a pale, freckle-faced boy in a dirty white sweat-shirt, a mop of brown, unwashed hair and a smear of ketchup on his chin. He put up a shaky hand to wipe it off and Carole screamed.

'There's blood! There's blood on your sleeve!'

'It's not blood, it's ketchup, you jerk,' said Greg.

But it was blood. Cal knew as he stared down at the red on his fingers. He looked at his wrist and there, just below the cuff of his sweat-shirt was a small neat cut with the blood just starting to congeal. He looked up at the window once more, staring out through his reflection to the street beyond—the busy street, crowded with tourists, with a Midland Red bus just pulling away from the stop outside the restaurant, people and parked cars . . . a summer's evening . . . He looked at his watch. Seven fifteen . . .

'Too much Shakespeare, I reckon,' said Gene caustically, 'gone to his head.'

Cal turned back to the table.

35

'Say, Lou, is there a play called *Love's Labour's Won?*' he asked abruptly.

'*Love's Labour's Lost*, you dumbhead,' she said amiably, glad to show off her knowledge.

'No, this is called *Love's Labour's Won*,' Cal insisted.

'No such thing.'

'Lou *knows*,' Greg said eagerly. 'She knows all the plays.'

'Where'd you hear it?' Lou asked.

Cal did not answer. How could you say that you had heard the name in a garden not ten minutes walk away, uttered in your hearing by the eleven-year-old son of the man who had written it . . . over four hundred years ago? They would cart him off to the medic for sure, and they'd be right. Probably put him on the next plane back home and that, Cal knew with a sudden certainty, was what he did not want. Cal wanted to stay—to stay and solve the mystery.

Chapter Four

The receiver crackled with interference and Cal moved it
further from his ear.

'Cal? You still there?'

'Yes, Mom, I'm still here.'

'You okay? You sound kinda distant.'

'I'm okay.'

'That's my baby. Well I gotta go. Got a date.'

There was a pause, but Cal said nothing.

'Cy's been sweet, Cal. You'll love him.'

'Who?'

'Cy. My attorney. I *told* you.'

Cal was silent.

'You getting on all right there?'

'Sure, Mom. Fine.'

'And the guys you're with? Good bunch of kids?'

'Sure. Great.'

'Soaking up the culture?'

'Yeah, Mom.'

'That's just fine.' There was a pause. 'So don't forget. If
your father does try to get in touch, you will give me a ring
straight away, won't you? It's important, Cal. I don't want
you upset by that son-of-a-bitch, you understand?'

A pause. 'Yeah. I understand.'

'Well, bye then, baby. Sure miss you. Be good.'

'Yeah. Bye, Mom.'

Cal carefully replaced the receiver and sat down on the
bottom step of the stairs. He rested his head against the
cool of the banister and tried to think.

His father. His father had been trying to contact him.
After all this time. Nine months, two weeks, three days.

37

That was when he had walked out of the house and since then, nothing. No phone call, no letter, no meeting. And now he had been ringing his school. Why?

Suppose, just suppose, he was trying to see him. How would he look? Cal tried to form a mental image. Nine months, two weeks, and three days is a long time. Would he have changed? Grown older? Would Cal even *recognize* his father, he wondered in a moment of panic? And if they did meet, what would his father say? What would *he* say? Cal shook his head. Crazy. It was crazy. He sighed and got to his feet, feeling tired and deflated. Slowly he went upstairs.

'As you can see, this theatre, The Swan, is similar to the kind of theatre in which Shakespeare and his contemporaries would have performed their plays. Elizabethan playhouses were round or octagonal, and the stage jutted right out into the audience, looking rather like an apron. Surrounding the stage at ground level was a yard where most of the audience would have stood to watch the performance.'

The guide from the Royal Shakespeare Theatre looked round the group, who were comfortably seated in the gallery. 'We don't expect our audiences to stand nowadays,' she added. 'In Shakespeare's day only the better-off would have had seats in the galleries which surrounded the yard.'

Cal's group looked down at the stage. The guide continued.

'Apart from the seating, there are one or two other differences between this theatre and the Elizabethan playhouses. Anyone like to guess what they are?'

'Would there have been a roof in Shakespeare's day?' Lou asked tentatively.

The guide looked approving. 'That's right. In Shakespeare's time, the stage would have been protected by a canopy and the galleries would have been roofed, but the yard area around the stage would have been open to the elements. Any other differences?' She looked hopefully at Lou, but Lou shook her head and no one else spoke.

'As you can see, the interior of this theatre is made of unpainted wood—Canadian pine. It was the result of a generous donation from a compatriot of yours from the United States, Mr Frederick Koch. Elizabethan theatres would also have been built of wood, but the interiors would have been painted. And this theatre holds a smaller audience than The Globe, or The Rose, or the other Elizabethan theatres. Any questions?'

'Would there have been a theatre like this in Stratford?' Cal asked suddenly, then blushed as the entire group, including John Loveday, turned to him in surprise.

'No. The only purpose-built playhouses were in London. There were many companies of actors—they were known as players—and they either performed in the playhouses or in the courtyards of inns and pubs, mostly just outside the City boundaries. During epidemics of the plague—and these happened quite regularly—the London playhouses were closed and the companies would then tour the country, performing in towns like Stratford, but the performances would have taken place in the street or in the courtyards of inns.' The guide got to her feet. 'I'll take you through to the main theatre. You'll see that it's very different from The Swan.'

The group rose and began to follow. But Cal hesitated for a moment. He leaned over the rail and looked down at the stage. The theatre seemed to glow with honey-coloured warmth.

'Father is a player with the Lord Chamberlain's Men. They are very good players.'

Hamnet's voice was so clear that Cal glanced round sharply.

39

'Cal!' John Loveday was standing by the swing doors. '*Must* you always be last?'

Cal gave one final puzzled glance round the empty theatre then followed John through the doors and into a wide passageway bounded on one side by the back of a stage set and on the other by a brick wall. Their guide stopped.

'This area is known as the back dock,' she explained. 'Behind the set is the main stage—I'll take you on to it in a moment. Behind this other wall is The Swan Theatre.' She pointed to the far end. 'Through there are the actors' dressing rooms and the Green Room—which is the name given to a kind of common room where the actors can relax.'

She moved towards a table. 'If you'll just come over here, you can see some of the props for this production. Do look, but please don't touch.'

The group clustered round the table but Cal was disinclined to join them. He was restless and on edge, finding it difficult to concentrate on what the guide was saying. Perhaps, he thought, he was about to return to the past. The thought sent a shiver down his back.

A sudden movement at the far end of the back dock caught Cal's attention. A man hurried through the swing doors and stopped abruptly at seeing so many people. He was a short, stocky man, with a square bearded face, dark hair, and deepset eyes. He was dressed in shirt and jeans and a jersey was slung casually around his shoulders. He glanced swiftly round the group and then grinned.

'Shepherding your flock, John?' he questioned in the clear, ringing tones of the professional actor.

John straightened up from the table. 'As you see.'

'I won't detain you then.' He gave a slightly mocking salute and came forwards. 'Excuse me, please,' he said, smiling charmingly at Carole who stood in his path. She moved out of his way and he went out through the stage door.

Carole watched him go then turned to John. 'Hey, was that an actor?' she demanded.

'Yes,' he said shortly.

'And you know him?'

'Yes.'

'Is he famous?'

John did not reply for a moment, then said softly, '"*Fame that all hunt after in their lives*".'

'Hey?'

John smiled somewhat sourly. 'A quotation from Shakespeare. *Love's Labour's Lost.*'

Cal glanced up at him. Carole sighed. 'Yeah, okay, sure, but is he famous?'

'That depends on your definition of fame.'

'Okay, okay. What's his name?'

'Wantage. Richard Wantage.'

'Never heard of him.' She grinned. 'Bit of a dish though, isn't he.'

Greg snorted and John hurried into action. 'Come on. We're keeping our guide waiting.'

The tour was completed at a fast pace, with John impatiently chivying everyone along. They were rushed at high speed on and off the main stage and soon deposited in the bookshop where their guide left them, after indicating the area containing costumes and props from the plays, which, she said, they were at liberty to try on. The group dived enthusiastically into the wicker baskets and were soon dressed in a motley assortment of clothes. John watched them a little sourly.

'Right,' he said at last, glancing at his watch. 'The coach leaves for London at 5 p.m. I shall expect you all to be waiting outside the guest house with your luggage at a quarter to. Until then, you're free to do what you want.'

Carole placed a crown upon her head. 'Do you think I'd make an actress, Mr Loveday?' She threw a cloak around her shoulders in a theatrical gesture. 'I could play opposite your dishy friend.' John raised his eyebrows and Carole slipped her arm through his. 'Come on, Mr Loveday, I'm only teasing. How about buying me a coffee and telling me more about the gorgeous Richard Wantage?' she asked persuasively.

'No thank you, Carole,' John said drily, disentangling his arm.

'Okay,' she replied equably. 'Come on, you guys, let's leave him in peace.'

She went back to the others. Cal, who had not taken part in the dressing up, saw John close his eyes for a second. He stepped forwards.

'Mr Loveday, sir.'

John turned wearily.

'Mind if I ask a couple of questions?'

'If you must,' John said discouragingly.

Cal came closer. 'Well, it's nothing important, it's just . . . did Shakespeare write a play called *Love's Labour's Won?*'

John looked at him in surprise. 'Let's go outside,' he said abruptly.

He led the way out into the bright sunshine.

'I think you mean *Love's Labour's Lost* don't you, Cal?'

Cal shook his head. 'Nope. I heard about that one already.'

John was silent for a moment. 'Is this some kind of a joke, Cal, because if it is . . .'

'Honest. I'm kind of curious. I heard there was this play, and I wondered about it.'

'Where did you hear of it?'

Cal shrugged and looked innocent. 'Just around . . .'

John stopped and stared at Cal. Suddenly he relaxed.

'Can it be, Cal, that the air of Stratford has at last penetrated to the inner depths?' he asked lightly. 'I

42

remember now, you asked a question in the theatre. I was impressed. Miracles do still happen.'

The sarcasm was lost on Cal. 'Did Shakespeare write that play?' he asked again, adding 'Sir' for good measure.

'It's a bit of an unresolved mystery,' John said seriously. He smiled disarmingly, looking suddenly much younger. 'As with anything to do with Shakespeare, Cal, there's much that's open to conjecture.'

He leaned against the wall. 'A play of that name *was* mentioned by a man called Francis Meres in a book published in 1598, *Palladis Tamia.* He wrote down a list of plays, among them *Love's Labour's Lost* and *Love's Labour's Won.* Some people hold that *Love's Labour's Won* was the original title of another play, such as *The Taming of the Shrew* or *All's Well that Ends Well. Much Ado about Nothing* is perhaps the best suggestion, but no one knows for certain.'

He seemed to forget Cal as he warmed to his theme. 'In the early 1950s a dealer in old books discovered an Elizabethan manuscript which had been used for binding a book of sermons. The manuscript was found to be part of a ledger of an early seventeenth century stationer, Sir Christopher Hunt, and contained notes, jottings—possibly a list or part of a list of the books in his shop. A number of plays were on that list, one of which was *Love's Labour's Won.* So that gives some confirmation that there *was* a play of that title in print in 1603, though whether by Shakespeare or by someone else is another matter. However it adds something in support of Meres.'

As he spoke his voice grew more intense. Cal noticed his hands, clenching and unclenching, the knuckles showing white.

'Would it be important?' he asked.

'What?'

'Well, if there was another play by Shakespeare?'

John slowly turned to him, his eyes almost feverishly bright.

43

'Important?' he repeated slowly. 'Important? If there *was* a play of that name by Shakespeare which has since been lost, and if, *if* it should ever be found . . .' he stopped.

'It'd be worth a lot of money, huh?' Cal finished.

'That, yes, an incalculable amount . . . but that's irrelevant,' he said, dismissively. 'It's the *literary* worth that's incalculable. That and the moment of finding, of possessing such a thing. That moment of glory. I'd give ten years of my life—no, more—if I could find something like that . . .'

'Is it likely?' Cal asked.

John stared at him, unseeing, then his eyes sharpened and narrowed, as if he had just got Cal into focus.

'Of course not,' he said curtly. 'It's just a dream.' He straightened himself abruptly.

'Hey, when was *Love's Labour's Lost* written?' Cal asked suddenly.

'This taste for scholarship, Cal—it's overwhelming,' John said drily. 'Now let me see . . . it was one of his early plays. Most probably around 1594 or 95.'

He hurried to the steps as if anxious to break off the conversation. Cal stayed where he was, lost in thought.

'I see, yeah, thanks,' he muttered slowly. John hesitated for a moment, glanced sharply at Cal, then turned, ran down the steps and was gone.

'Psst!'

A figure reared up from the foot of the steps. It was Nicky. She put her finger to her lips and disappeared from view. Cal watched her run, crouching, round the side of the theatre and towards the river. He grinned and followed at a more leisurely pace. Once round the corner Nicky straightened up.

'Hi.'

'Hi yourself.'

'You didn't know I was there, did you?' she asked anxiously.

44

'Nope.'

'Good. C'mon. Let's have an ice-cream.'

They wandered across the grass to the ice-cream stand and did not speak until they had both made their purchases. Cal snatched quick sidelong glances at Nicky. Out of school uniform, she looked older than he remembered.

'How did you know where I'd be?' he asked curiously, unwrapping his choc-ice.

Nicky chased a piece of pink ice-cream that was sliding down the outside of her cone before replying.

'S'easy. All tours follow the same pattern.' She glanced at him over the top of her ice-cream. 'Anyway, I have private sources of information. Said I was going to be a detective didn't I?'

'Yeah.'

They walked towards the bridge in silence.

'Why aren't you at school?' Cal asked suddenly.

'Day off.'

Cal looked surprised.

'Honest. I'm not playing truant.' She finished her ice-cream and gave a final lick round her lips. 'We get odd days off in the year so that the teachers can sit around and talk about us.' Cal was sceptical. 'It's true—cross my heart and hope to die!' She looked at him. 'So—how's life?'

Cal did not answer. They crossed the bridge and walked down to the waterside. Relaxed holiday-makers strolled along the bank, and swans, ducks, and boats shared the serenity of the river. The sun glinted on the surface . . . It was peaceful and timeless . . . Had much changed since Shakespeare's day?

Should he tell Nicky? No. It was too crazy. No one would, no one *could*, believe him.

He sat on the bank and she sat beside him.

'What's happened?' she asked.

45

'What do you mean?'

'Something's happened, hasn't it?' she said. 'Don't tell me if you don't want but I wish you would. Perhaps I can help.'

Cal shrugged. 'I don't know.'

'Neither do I unless you tell me.'

Cal was silent.

'I'm *dying* of curiosity,' she said helpfully.

Cal glanced at her. 'You'll think I've gone crazy,' he began. 'I think I've gone crazy myself.'

Nicky was quiet as Cal poured out the whole story. She just listened and Cal was grateful. At first he spoke fast, words tumbling over themselves in the relief of speaking about it. But his voice slowed as he came to the end.

' . . . so there I was, back in McDonald's.' He paused for a moment. 'But there was this cut. See . . .' He held out his wrist so that she could see the small red mark, now almost healed. 'That's the only thing I've got to show that it really *did* happen and I've not gone crazy.' He looked down at the ground. 'But I don't suppose anyone'd believe me.'

There was a long silence. Then she sighed.

'It's not fair is it?'

'Hey?'

'Well, I'm a genuine hundred per cent Stratfordian born and bred. A real Warwickshire lass, "Made in England" stamped right through me. And who are you? An American tourist, here today and gone back home tomorrow. And who has the adventure? It's my town, yet you're the one to get the excitement—it's just not fair.' She mused silently for a moment. 'You don't know how lucky you are.'

'Lucky?' Cal exclaimed. 'Lucky? It was just . . . horrible . . . frightening. Look, perhaps it never happened. Perhaps I was sick or something and dreamt it.'

'But you don't believe that.'

'No.'

46

Nicky stared moodily at the swans. 'Wish I could go back in time.'

'Well, there's nothing I can do about it. I can't control it. It might never happen again.'

'Oh, I think it will.'

'You do?' Cal was startled by the certainty in her voice.

'Oh yes. I'm sure of it.'

'So you do believe me . . . you do believe it happened.'

'You couldn't make up anything like that.' She gave him a sidelong glance. 'You don't know enough about that period of history do you? Besides, *"There are more things in heaven and earth, Horatio, than are dreamt of in your philosophy"*.'

'What's that?'

She grinned wickedly. 'Shakespeare.'

Cal laughed. He suddenly felt as if a weight had been lifted from him.

'Anyway, even if I can't go back in time, I can still help, can't I?' she said practically.

'How?'

'Well, I can find things out. I'm very good at finding things out.'

'Okay.' Cal stood up. 'We're off to London this evening, but we'll be back Saturday. Perhaps we can meet someplace?'

'Sure. I'll find you.'

'Where do you live?'

'Old Town. But don't worry. I know where you're staying.'

'How d'you know that?'

She laughed. 'You don't expect me to give away all my secrets do you? Bye!' Then she was gone, running along the riverbank and disappearing among the trees. Cal watched her go, then turned the other way and slowly returned towards the town.

Nicky arrived home hot and dishevelled. She erupted through the front door and shouted up the stairs.

47

'Anyone in?'

The door at the top of the landing opened and her brother appeared, a holdall in his hand. Nicky hung on to the bottom of the banisters, panting for breath. 'Glad I haven't missed you.'

Her brother gazed down at her. 'God, you look a mess,' he said disgustedly. 'Wherever have you been?'

Nicky ignored this. 'You've got to tell me all about a play of Shakespeare's!' she demanded.

He descended the stairs. 'Is this for school, because I've told you before, Nicky, I'm not doing your homework for you.'

She pulled a face. 'Don't be so stuffy.'

'And I'm in a hurry.'

'It's not for school. It's for a friend.' She grinned. 'Someone you know.'

He raised his eyebrows and looked at her consideringly. 'Make me a cup of coffee then and I'll give you five minutes.'

She pulled a face. 'Bribery will get you everywhere.'

She disappeared into the kitchen and put on the kettle. 'Where's Mum?'

He followed her, shrugging his shoulders. 'Working late? Stuck in the traffic? How should I know? I'm not her keeper, thank God. I've enough to do keeping track of a group of spoiled American kids.'

Nicky gave him a sidelong glance. 'And you're off to London this evening and you'll be back on Saturday.'

'How do you know that?'

'I have my spies,' she said then laughed. 'Well, one spy exactly. You'll know him. His name's Cal.'

'Oh. Him.' John Loveday frowned.

Nicky grinned. 'You're not his flavour-of-the-month either. Know what he calls you?'

'I can imagine,' John said curtly.

'Well, I'm not going to tell you.'

48

Nicky poured boiling water on to the coffee and added milk. She put sugar into one of the mugs and stirred it vigorously, slopping coffee over the sides. John watched her, still frowning.

'How did you meet him?' he asked abruptly.

Nicky shrugged. 'Just chance. I was coming home from school. He doesn't know that you're my big brother.'

'Why not?'

'Because I haven't told him. It's more fun that way.'

John took the cup from her impatiently.

'Look, Nicky, I'm not getting tied up in one of your childish games.'

'Look, Nicky, I'm not getting tied up in one of your childish games,' she mimicked. 'It's not childish and it's not a game. It's a really amazing thing. I don't suppose you'll believe it but I do.'

'You'd believe anything.'

'No, I wouldn't. I've got a very suspicious nature.' She shepherded him out of the kitchen and into the lounge. 'I said I'd find something out for him and you're the best person to ask. What can you tell me about a play called *Love's Labour's Won?*'

John put down his mug and turned to her.

'Just what is this?'

'What?'

John looked at her steadily. 'Why does Cal want to know?'

'It's a secret . . . at least,' Nicky wrinkled her forehead. 'I'm not sure it's a secret. He never *said* that I wasn't to tell . . . at least . . . I don't think so . . .'

John drank his coffee and started to get up. 'While you're wrestling with the finer points of your conscience, your five minutes are ticking away.'

Nicky flushed. 'I hate you when you talk like that.'

John was silent and sat down again. 'All right,' he said at last. 'We'll do a deal. You tell me why Cal is so anxious to

49

know about *Love's Labour's Won* and I'll tell you all I know about the play.'

'Well . . .' Nicky hedged.

John smiled at her. 'Oh come on, Nicky, you can trust me with your secrets can't you? If they *are* secrets. I promise I'll believe anything you say. Cross my heart and all that.'

Nicky smiled back and kicked off her shoes. Sometimes, she thought, her older brother was still quite human, despite being at University and boringly clever. She settled herself comfortably on the settee.

Chapter Five

London was okay, Cal thought, as he stood on London Bridge and watched the ships sailing up and down the River Thames. He had enjoyed their whirlwind tour of the capital city: the Tower of London, Buckingham Palace, the Palace of Westminster, Oxford Street, Piccadilly. It had all been . . . he hunted for the right word . . . okay. He looked at the famous skyline and screwed up his eyes as he tried to make out some of the landmarks.

Some day, he thought, he would come back and do it properly, taking his time. His father would enjoy planning such a trip, reading up about the places beforehand so that he could answer Cal's questions. He would probably know the answers to most of them anyway—he was, after all, a lecturer in history and a good one at that, Cal thought loyally. He could make the past exciting, make it come alive for Cal, in a way that no one else could—not like 'The Stiff' who reeled off facts and figures in a dry and boring way. Cal had liked history. He had been good at it. But he had lost interest when his father went.

The skyline shimmered in the afternoon sun. Funny, thought Cal, he'd always heard that it rained in England. Rain and fog, that's what he'd been told. But it wasn't true. The weather had so far been perfect—too hot really to go trailing round old buildings.

It was too hot now, Cal thought, uncomfortably so . . . he could feel the sweat dripping down his face and his shirt was wet through . . .

. . . and getting wetter by the minute. The skyline disappeared behind a curtain of rain and the river turned sleet grey.

51

A hand on his shoulder made him jump.

'Found you at last, Master Cal! And a fine dance you've led me!'

Cal turned sharply.

He was confronted by a stout man with a round, mild-looking face, a mop of brown hair, and short, bedraggled beard. The man was dressed in worn clothes and wore a much-darned cloak, firmly clasped at the neck. Behind the man, a row of houses leaned inwards towards the cobbled street, the upper stories almost meeting the row on the opposite side. The view from the bridge was gone. The sudden shock made Cal catch his breath. He felt sick and panic-stricken and his legs buckled under him. The man caught him in a reassuringly strong grip.

'Too much cheap ale, is it?' the man said drily. 'I might have guessed. Don't worry, lad, Master Burbage will soon beat it out of you. Now make haste, we're late enough as it is!'

He tightened his grip on Cal and hurried him down the narrow street and off the bridge. Cal went unresisting, too bewildered to protest.

Once over the bridge the man set a fast pace, weaving his way through narrow streets, pushing past people, carts, and animals, while still keeping his tight hold on Cal's arm. Rain beat on Cal's unprotected head and splashed from the overhanging upper stories of the houses. The streets were awash and the bursting sewers spread their unpleasant contents over the cobbles and around their feet. A rat, wet fur sleeked down, scurried from one side of the street to the other. Cal shivered and the man glanced at him.

'Someone ought to knock some sense into you lads—going off in your shirt and hose and with the sky as black as the devil. Here.' He stopped, and, to Cal's amazement, took off his cloak and slung it round Cal's shoulders. 'That'll keep the worst off you.'

52

'But . . . gee . . . I can't . . .' Cal protested, trying to remove it with wet fumbling fingers.

'Do as you're told. Can't have you losing your voice, now can I? Fine book-keeper I'd be.'

He set off again, dragging Cal with him. 'So you went with the other lads to see the new playhouse, did you? A marvel, isn't it? They told me you'd been with them and said you'd slipped off down Bankside. But they couldn't fool Thomas Vincent—I know the tricks those rascals play on new apprentices. Left you in the alehouse I suppose and hoped you'd lose your way back, you being new to the City. I gave them short shrift before setting out. Any more games like that, I said, and I'd bang their silly heads together.'

Cal glanced at him, surprised. Despite his appearance, Thomas Vincent had an air of authority. Thomas caught his look.

'You'll see, lad, if you stay long enough, that we don't allow our apprentices to overstep the mark—and that goes for you as well as the others.' A fleeting smile spread across his face. 'You look like a cross between a drowned rat and something the cat's sicked up. White as a sheet. If you're going to vomit, kindly take my cloak off first. It might be old, but it's the only one I've got.'

He walked faster. 'What did you think of The Swan Theatre? Not bad, eh? Better than The Rose, don't you think? Master Henslowe's a worried man from what I hear. He's anxious about the competition, although "The Admiral's Men" are a passable company and he should have naught to fear. None of them a patch on "The Lord Chamberlain's Men", of course,' he finished with some pride.

Cal shook his head in total confusion and said nothing.

They had left the narrow streets behind and were walking down a muddy track which led across a field. Ahead of them was a large circular building and Thomas led the way round the outside wall until he reached a low door.

'In you go, lad and make haste into your costume. You're not late and no one should have missed you, though they're doubtless all running round clacking for me like a lot of headless chickens.'

He chuckled as he pushed Cal inside. Cal stood on the threshold of the room and stared in amazement. It was a large room, full of people, noise, and colour. Clothes lay everywhere, heaped on the floor, strewn on trestle tables, and piled in and around large wooden chests. Satins, velvets, brocades, glints of gold and silver thread, fine linen shirts, and delicate lacework were jumbled indiscriminately with humbler costumes in more sober colours.

It was a bit like some kind of a crazy clothes store, Cal thought, as he watched those in the room trying on the different clothes, discarding some, adjusting others, all to the accompaniment of much talking, laughter, and calls for help from a thin, worried-looking man.

'Peter, this doublet fits very ill. Very ill indeed. Have you no larger?'

'Peter, come here! This cloak is a vile colour, I cannot wear it!'

'Peter, aid me with these pumps. I can't . . . seem . . . to get them on my feet . . .' this said by a fat man with much puffing and blowing.

Peter darted here and there, placating, commiserating, adjusting, and adapting as he went.

There were no women in the room and Cal watched fascinated as a slim youth transformed himself into a girl by means of a dress of fine white lawn studded with hundreds of small silver jewels that winked and shimmered as he moved. He stuffed his fine fair hair into an elaborate wig and the change was completed. Peter carefully placed a fragile silver crown on his head, stood back and nodded critically.

54

'Aye, you'll do, Master Gilburne, not a bad Titania.'

Not everyone was trying on clothes. Two men practised sword-fighting on the far side of the room and a small group were in earnest conversation by the door. An elderly man muttered under his breath as he stared at large dog-eared sheets of paper hung on a nail, while an extraordinarily thin man with a worried frown on his face added to the general confusion by throwing more costumes out of one of the chests.

The only oasis of calm seemed to be where a man was sitting quietly on the edge of an opened chest of costumes. He was simply dressed, not in costume, and had a straight nose and neatly trimmed moustache and beard. His brown hair receded from his high, domed forehead. A quill pen was in his hand and a horn of ink was perched rather precariously beside him. The man seemed oblivious of the noise around him.

Thomas surveyed the scene from the doorway. Then he took a step inside. Faces were turned towards him and an instant clamour arose.

'Thomas! At last! We wait for rehearsal!'

'My lute has gone missing, Thomas—have you seen it?'

'Master Vincent, I was not able to get fresh rushes—can we use the old ones? They look well enough, but they smell foul.'

'Thomas! My speech in Act One. Someone—and I make no accusations—has changed it and it now reads most vilely!'

One of the sword-fighters, a tall dark man with a commanding face, turned and pointed his sword threateningly at the last speaker. 'If you are accusing me, Master Cundall . . .'

'Masters, masters!' Thomas pushed the sword harmlessly up into the air and the noise ceased.

He turned first to Master Cundall. 'If your speech has changed, it is a matter between you and Master

55

Shakespeare, no other player is involved.' He looked at the sword-fighters. 'And, good sirs, please, there is to be no sword-fighting in the tiring house. You know the rules, Master Burbage.'

The tall man grinned and bowed and handed Thomas his sword. Thomas laid it carefully on a bench before turning to the very thin man. 'Your lute, Master Gilbert, is doubtless where it was last night when you were entertaining us—at your lodgings.'

'The rushes, master . . .'

'Yes, John, we will use the old rushes for today's performance, but mind you get fresh for tomorrow.'

He went over to the man working quietly on the manuscript and moved the ink to a safer place. 'If you please, sir, *not* so near the costumes. You remember the accident we had last year on *Romeo and Juliet*.'

He turned and raised his voice to include everyone. 'This room is a disgrace, masters! A disgrace!' He began to bustle around, tidying away costumes and sorting props. 'Look to your costumes, Peter, these gentlemen will trample them into rags! Come, sirs, we are pressed for time—on stage please for rehearsal!'

Grumbling and muttering, the occupants of the room allowed themselves to be shepherded out through a far doorway, which was covered by a curtain. As he followed, Thomas glanced back at Cal.

'Peter, help Master Cal into his costume and be quick about it.'

Three boys, about Cal's age, lingered at the doorway. They were dressed in extravagant costumes and looked like bright, exotic flowers. The first, a stout lad, was sweating uncomfortably in a tightly fitting pink satin doublet and hose. He wore a large ruff around his neck and a white petal-shaped cap on his head. The second, who was tall and thin, was wearing a cape of snakeskins and his thin arms

56

and legs, dressed in green, stuck out from underneath. The third was resplendent in blue, stitched in a cobweb design, with silver threads. Cal thought they all looked ridiculous.

The one dressed in blue returned his look and grinned amiably.

'Did you enjoy your tour of the sights?' He turned to the boy in pink. 'Our wanderer found his way home, Ned.'

'Aye,' said Ned, who was finding it difficult to speak due to the tightness of his costume and his oversized ruff. His face was very red. 'Looks a bit the worse for wear, doesn't he?'

The first boy chortled. 'So do you, Ned. You'll die in that costume!'

The third boy frowned warningly. 'Peace, Hubert. We'll be heard on stage.'

They turned away from Cal and peered through the curtain. Apart from a distant murmur of voices, it was suddenly quiet in the room.

Peter approached, holding out some clothes. 'Come now, young master, quick as you can.'

Cal hesitantly pulled off his shirt. Peter took it, tut-tutting at its wetness. 'Catch your death, you will, like as not. Here.' He threw Cal a rough cloth. 'Dry yourself first.'

Cal dressed slowly, fumbling with the unfamiliar garments. Peter knelt and put soft grey shoes with long upturned points on his feet. He threw a short yellow cloak around his shoulders and placed a yellow and grey hat on his head.

'You'll do,' he said somewhat sourly. 'Now get along while I sort out the mess you fine players have made.'

He turned his back on Cal, who looked round, uncertainly. Hubert turned to him.

'They're nearing our cue—are you ready?'

'Um . . . sure . . .'

Ned held the curtain and Cal looked out on to the back of the stage. In front of him were two actors; the youth in the white dress and a man who was lying on a rushes-strewn bench. The head and shoulders of the man were hidden inside a huge model head of a donkey. For a moment Cal forgot where he was.

'Say, who's that?' he asked.

'Who, Bottom?' the thin boy replied. 'His name is Philip Sturley. He has been hired while Master Kempe is sick.'

'They say he is good, John,' said Hubert.

Cal stared at the actors for a moment then looked round. The stage jutted into the centre of the circular building. A wooden canopy protected it from the weather, but the surrounding yard was open to the sky and it was still raining, spattering down on to the heads of the small groups of people who were standing there.

A sharp push in the small of his back propelled him out of the doorway. Cal ran on to the stage with the three boys.

'*Ready*,' called John, taking off his green cap with a flourish and executing a courtiers' deep bow.

'*And I*,' called Hubert, bowing in turn.

There was silence. Faces turned to Cal, who looked nervously round the stage.

'*And I*,' came a quiet voice from a corner. Cal saw Thomas, seated on a stool, a manuscript on his knee.

'Go on, go on,' called an impatient voice from the yard.

Ned called, '*And I*,' and the three chorused, '*Where shall we go?*'

Titania spoke and the boys crossed the stage, following rehearsed moves. Cal remained where he was, rooted to the spot. He had once taken part in a play at school—that had been bad enough, he thought fleetingly, but this was a thousand times worse.

John spoke again, bowing to Bottom. '*Hail, mortal!*'

Hubert bowed. '*Hail!*'

Again silence followed by Thomas's whispered prompt: '*Hail!*'

There was movement from the yard.

'Stop. Stop the rehearsal!'

A man crossed the yard and jumped lightly up on to the stage with a swirl of his short cloak, scattering raindrops about him. Cal recognized him as the man who had been seated quietly in the tiring house, engrossed in a manuscript. The man was anything but quiet now and his expressive brown eyes were angry.

'You, sirrah!' He beckoned to Cal curtly. 'You are out of your part!'

Cal swallowed hard.

'What is your name?'

'Cal . . . Calvin . . . sir . . .'

The man grasped Cal's arm. 'You have but a minor part, just two lines. There is, surely, no great difficulty in memorizing those two lines?'

'N . . . no, sir.'

'Then why, in the name of heaven, can you not remember them?'

Cal was silent and the man turned, exasperated, towards the silent audience in the yard. 'Richard! Have you aught to say to this—this bedraggled specimen of humanity, this flea-ridden apology of a youth who thinks to become a player?'

The tall man whom Cal had seen sword-fighting in the tiring house moved to the foot of the stage.

'Peace, Will—'tis not so very serious a fault. The lad is new.'

The man released Cal's arm and sighed. 'Perhaps you have forgotten, Richard, that we perform this play tomorrow afternoon and it is the one to be played at Court?'

'I have not forgotten.'

The man looked at Cal. 'Well?' he said sternly.

Cal glanced down at the dirty rushes strewn over the floor of the stage.

'The part of Moth is hardly arduous and we have rehearsed it.'

Cal felt absurdly ashamed of himself. 'I'm sorry, sir,' he said miserably.

There was a moment's silence. 'Let it pass for now.' The man lifted Cal's chin, forcing him to look up. 'Although you must have both words and actions for the performance, otherwise we shall have to send you home. You do understand that we cannot tolerate laziness in this company?'

He looked sharply across to where Hubert and Ned were standing, sniggering behind their hands. 'There is nothing whatsoever to laugh at in another player's misfortune,' he said coldly.

He glanced round at the silent gathering. 'We will leave this scene for now,' he said crisply. 'Thomas, we will rehearse the removal of the ass's head.'

'Very good, Master Shakespeare,' Thomas said, thumbing through the well-worn sheets of his manuscript.

Shakespeare turned back to Cal.

'Stand here, Cal,' he said in a gentler voice. 'You will be relieved to know that I have given Moth no lines in this scene.' Cal looked up. The anger was gone and the dark, expressive eyes that watched him so closely were warm and understanding. Cal flushed and Shakespeare smiled wryly. 'I know the kind of games apprentices play and I saw your bedraggled entrance into the tiring house. Richard is right. You are new. I should not have berated you so.' He held Cal's look gravely for a moment then, with a slight bow, said simply, 'I crave your pardon.' With that he jumped lightly off the stage and returned to his position at the far side of the yard.

The scene began, but Cal paid no attention to it. So that was Shakespeare, he thought. The father of Susanna, Hamnet, and Judith. The most famous playwright of all time, the one whose native town was visited by thousands upon thousands of sightseers each year. And that was the man who had given his new play to his son—the play that had been lost or stolen, the one Cal was somehow supposed to find.

Cal watched Shakespeare stand in the yard, listening attentively as the scene progressed. What an amazing guy, Cal thought. Fancy him apologizing like that, in front of everyone, just as if Cal had been someone who mattered. It took a big guy to do something like that. A really big guy.

And he had been right to get angry, Cal reflected. I would have been angry if it had been my play and some two-bit actor had forgotten the words. He could understand why it was that Hamnet did not want to worry him with the loss of the manuscript and Susanna was so fiercely proud of him. I'd be proud too, Cal thought. Who wouldn't be?

'Philip. A word.'

Once again Shakespeare jumped up on to the stage. Bottom turned his ass's head towards him and the actor carefully lifted the heavy weight from his shoulders with an audible sigh of relief.

Philip Sturley was a thickset man with a plain round face and mop of red hair. Beads of sweat ran down his forehead and into his short thick beard. He put down the ass's head and wiped his forehead with his hand.

Shakespeare spoke quietly. When he had finished, Sturley hesitated for a moment then nodded his head.

'Yes, master.'

'Good.' Shakespeare turned to the rest of the players. 'We will take the line from, *"Where's Mounsieur Mustardseed?"*.'

Philip took up the ass's head and Cal watched him, wondering how anyone could act with something so heavy over his head. As he watched he saw Philip glance at Shakespeare, who had returned to his place in the yard. The look startled Cal, for it was one of barely controlled anger followed immediately by a small sly smile of triumph. Then the ass's head came down over the man's face.

61

'Our new man takes criticism ill,' Hubert murmured in his ear.

'*Sleep thou, and I will wind thee in my arms.*

Fairies, be gone, and be all ways away.'

Cal was prodded sharply into action by John. Obediently he followed the three boys into the tiring house where he stood just inside the door, watching the action on stage.

Titania and Oberon were standing beside Bottom who appeared to be asleep on the bench.

Titania raised her hand. '*Music, ho, music, such as charmeth sleep!*'

There was silence on the stage and Shakespeare called out sharply, 'Music! Wake up there!'

A small voice called from high above Cal's head. 'Sorry, Master Shakespeare, Master Gilbert's gone back to his lodging to fetch his lute!'

Shakespeare closed his eyes for a moment. 'Heaven deliver us!'

Thomas stirred on his stool. 'Come, sirs,' he said mildly, but with authority, 'we must finish this scene and make ready for the afternoon's performance. We shall do without the music. We'll begin from your line, Samuel, "*Music, ho, music*". Are you ready to remove the ass's head, Nicholas?'

A small, wiry actor, dressed in Puck's red and yellow costume, nodded his head.

Titania repeated the line while Puck stepped behind the actor asleep on the bench.

'*Now when thou wakest with thine own fool's eyes peep.*'

He bent down and lifted the dummy head and the scene was soon ended.

Thomas got up from his stool. 'Thank you, sirs. We have no more time this morning. Would the players performing in *Love's Labour's Lost* this afternoon please remain.'

The actors relaxed and a buzz of chatter arose from the yard.

'Samuel, we must arrange your wig better,' Shakespeare said briskly, returning to the stage. 'It sits most uncomfortably and I am fearful of it blowing away during the performance.'

'The groundlings would be amused,' Samuel replied, removing the crown then the wig.

'No doubt.' Shakespeare smiled. 'Especially when they beheld a bald-headed Queen Titania left on stage.'

'Faith, I'm not bald-headed!' Samuel protested. 'I have a fine head of hair.'

'Aye, 'tis so fine, we can scarce see it,' Shakespeare retorted drily. Samuel laughed and Shakespeare turned to the book-keeper. 'Thomas, a word or two about the props before you go.'

'Aye, master.'

'Now, Philip,' Shakespeare said earnestly, taking the actor by the arm. 'It is most important that you speak no more than is set down. Otherwise you will confuse your fellow players and lose the thread of the piece. Whatever has been acceptable among the companies for whom you have worked, is not acceptable by "The Lord Chamberlain's Men". There is to be no extemporizing. That is an absolute rule here.'

'Yes, master.'

Shakespeare must have caught the undertone of resentment, for he spoke in a softer voice.

'You do well, Philip, and I would have you do even better. Come, we will talk more of this later.'

He clapped the actor on the shoulder and went swiftly into the tiring house, Thomas at his heels. Cal watched from the doorway as Philip, alone on the stage, hesitated for a moment. A deep red flush mottled his face and his hands clenched and unclenched. Then he laughed.

'Yes, master, no, master, three bags full, master. Well, I've a little trick up my sleeve for you, Master Shakespeare.'

He caught Cal's eye.

'What are you gawping at, fool?' he said brusquely.

He brushed past Cal, knocking him to one side. Cal stared after him with interest, then followed him thoughtfully into the tiring house.

Chapter Six

The flag flew from the top of The Theatre; the trumpets sounded; the play was about to begin.

People were still hurrying along the muddy path across the field in order to join the hundreds who were already crammed inside. The rain had stopped and the sun was shining. Cal, his distinctive costume hidden by a long black cloak which he had taken from the tiring house, mingled with the excited crowds in the yard, his eyes fixed on the stage.

Since the end of rehearsal he had kept watch on Philip Sturley. He had hung around the tiring house until Sturley had changed out of his costume, then shadowed him out of the building and over to an inn. He had followed him inside, keeping close to the wall, but nobody had taken the slightest notice of him. He had watched as Sturley did nothing more blameworthy than share a jug of ale with some cronies, then followed him back to The Theatre and waited in the tiring house while he dressed in the costume of Costard. Only when Thomas had called the players on stage did Cal feel free to wander round to the yard and join the crowds.

A thrill of anticipation rustled through the audience and the play began.

Cal, to his surprise, enjoyed it. Standing in the warm sunshine, part of a vast and sympathetic crowd who were alternately cheering, booing, hissing, and clapping at the play's twists and turns, Cal was entranced, and cheered and clapped as loudly as anyone when the players came to the front of the stage to take their bows.

Sturley took a solo bow. He was good, Cal thought uncritically, and cheered with the rest of the audience. The players left the stage and the audience began to move towards the exits. Cal pushed past them and slipped around the outer walls to take up a position outside the door to the tiring house.

He did not have long to wait. Sturley soon appeared in the company of a group of players. Cal followed them across the field and watched, at a safe distance, as Sturley's companions loudly tried to persuade him to go with them to a drinking party. He declined, and eventually they went off, while Sturley turned and plunged into a narrow maze of streets.

Cal trailed after him anxiously. He kept far too close as he was worried about losing him, but the actor gave no sign of knowing that he was being followed. He walked fast and Cal scurried behind, cursing the over-large cloak and ridiculously pointed shoes he wore, both of which threatened to trip him up at every step.

Sturley turned a corner. Cal hurriedly followed him into a narrow alleyway. The actor had disappeared. Cal stopped and looked around, biting his lip. The alley seemed to lead straight into a blank wall. He walked slowly, looking from side to side. Tall, overhanging houses were pressed together in a continuous row, their doors closed. It was very quiet. Suddenly he spotted a narrow gap. A flight of worn steps led down to a stone jetty and beyond it was the reflection of light on water. He could see nothing of Sturley but, at the foot of the steps, an inn sign hung motionless in the still early evening air.

Cautiously Cal made his way down the steps and peered in through the window. The glass was thick with grime and, at first, Cal could see little except the outline of figures in the dark interior. Then Sturley's face swam into view and, for a fraction of time, they stared at one another. Cal drew back, sweating.

So what if he has seen me? Cal reasoned to himself, trying to stop his heart from thumping. It's a public place, after all.

No one came out of the inn and, after what seemed an age of anxious waiting, Cal slowly edged back to his former position.

Sturley was seated at a table. He was talking to someone who was hidden behind a high wooden settle. Cal strained his ears but could hear nothing of their conversation. He thought of creeping past the window and sliding just inside the door, but gave up the idea as too risky.

Then Sturley's partner stood and Cal could see him clearly. He was a thin man with high cheekbones set in a gaunt face. His eyes were dark and close-set. His hair was black and long and he was dressed all in black. He pulled back his cloak and took out a package which he placed on the table. Sturley looked at it slowly, picked it up, and put it inside his doublet. He looked up at the man, nodded and spoke. The man facing him turned to go.

Cal moved swiftly. He left the window and sat down on a step, pulling the hood of his cloak well over his head. Hopefully the man would think him either drunk or asleep. He leaned against the wall and closed his eyes. He heard slow, deliberate footsteps approach, pause, then pass on up the steps to the street. A cloak brushed against Cal's legs.

Should he stay with Sturley or go after the stranger? Cal pushed his hood back and watched the cloaked figure reach the top of the steps and turn the corner. Still undecided, he stood up.

Strong arms clamped him from behind. He was lifted off his feet, his hood pulled over his face and he was carried, struggling and half-suffocating, inside the inn. The grip around his waist tightened.

'Hold still, you little devil!' said a rough voice close to his ear.

He was carried up some stairs, there was a pause while a door was opened, and he was thrown to the floor. For a moment he was too shaken to move.

'Let's have a look at you.'

Cal slowly pushed back the hood with a trembling hand. Facing him, seated astride a chair, was Philip Sturley.

'Well, well, well.'

He put out his hand and jerked Cal's cloak off him.

'A moth, no less,' he said sourly. He stared at Cal, his round, heavy face expressionless. 'What were you doing?'

'M-me? N-nothing . . .' Cal stuttered.

'Oh yes you were, little moth. You were flying too close to the window. Trying to get in, were you, to overhear the conversation?' He grabbed Cal's wrist and twisted it, hard.

'You know what happens to moths that fly too close, don't you? They burn their wings.' Cal looked up at him. His expression was ugly and his grip on Cal's wrist painful. 'I remember now,' he said slowly. 'You were on stage spying on me at the end of rehearsal.' He twisted Cal's wrist again. 'Come, I am in haste, and I want the truth. Who are you spying for?'

'N-no one. Hey, let go, you're hurting.'

'I'll hurt you far worse if you lie,' Sturley said grimly. 'I ask you again—who are you spying for?'

'No one! I'm not a spy and I'm not spying for anyone, so take your grubby hands off me!'

'You work for yourself, do you?' Sturley looked contemptuously at Cal. 'You're lying, of course.' He paused, but Cal did not say anything.

'Very well, let that rest for the moment.' Sturley's voice hardened. 'What did you see and what did you hear?'

'Nothing,' Cal said. 'The window was too dirty,' he added lamely.

Sturley laughed shortly and released Cal. 'Well for you,' he said. 'So why were you there at all?'

Cal sat up. 'No reason,' he said, trying to sound sullen but truthful. 'I just fancied a stroll.'

'No?' Sturley stared hard at him. 'So you hung around the tiring house, for no reason? You followed me across the field, also for no reason? You chose to let my friends go their ways and selected me for your target as you followed me to this inn—for no reason other than that the evening was bright and you "fancied a stroll"?'

Cal was silent. He glanced round the room, which was sparsely furnished.

'You approve my lodgings,' Sturley said sarcastically. 'Good, for you will have to spend some time here.' He stood up, pulled Cal roughly to his feet and thrust him into the chair.

He turned his back, and Cal, grasping the opportunity, leapt up and made a lunge for the door. He was not fast enough. Sturley was there before him, a dagger in one hand, a rope in the other and a very unpleasant expression on his face. He moved towards Cal, who backed away nervously.

'Don't you know,' said Sturley, forcing him back to the chair, 'that moths never escape?' Cal stumbled and Sturley pushed him down. He pulled his arms behind him and bound them securely at the wrists then he tied his legs to the chair and put a rag around his mouth.

'I must apologize for my lack of hospitality,' he said sarcastically, 'but you came upon me unawares.'

He turned the chair so that it faced the wall. Cal could hear him moving around the room.

'I have a pressing engagement, otherwise we should have enjoyed a fruitful talk. I will have the truth from you, little moth, and not a string of lies. Still, you are in no hurry, are you? I dare swear you will not be missed. You will stay until my return.'

There was the sound of a drawer opening, then a click as it closed and was locked.

'And when I return, you will be a little tired, a little hungry, and a great deal more forthcoming.'

Footsteps came towards the chair and Sturley jerked Cal's head backwards. He felt the prick of a dagger at his throat and Sturley stared down at him, an unreadable expression on his face.

'For you know what happens to spies, don't you? They are found in ditches with their throats slit.' He shifted the angle of the dagger slightly and Cal swallowed convulsively. 'Or they are washed ashore with the tide, their bodies bloated and unrecognizable.' He paused. 'The river is but a few feet from this door.' He stared at Cal for what seemed an age. 'Think on it.'

The pressure of the dagger was increased for a moment, then withdrawn. Cal heard swift footsteps cross the room, the door was opened and closed and a key turned in the lock.

Cal closed his eyes. The ropes cut into his arms and legs and the gag made him feel sick. His stomach churned and he felt faint. Perhaps he would return to the present, he thought hopefully. He kept his eyes closed and willed himself back . . .

. . . back to where? He began to panic as he could not remember where he had been when he had gone into the past. It was all a blank. He struggled and pain made him open his eyes. It was getting dark and shadows played on the rough-plastered wall in front of him. Cal shivered.

Lousy detective I am, he thought. Nicky would have stalked the guy better. He could have kicked himself for being such a fool. It looked so easy on TV and in the movies. First hint of a problem and they're into their cars and on to their mobile phones for help.

Cars, thought Cal, in fresh panic. That was in the twentieth century, along with television and Nicky and everything he understood. Where would help come from in this horrible place? Cal began to struggle again. There must be some way, he thought, straining against his bonds and trying not to notice how they cut into him. There *must* be some way of getting free.

He wriggled harder and the chair rocked. Cal stopped, the panic subsiding. Hey, wait a minute, he thought. Wait a minute. If I can just rock this chair around, I might get somewhere. Cautiously, he tested his theory. With care he could do it. Rock too hard and the chair could overturn. Rock slowly and it moved. With a sense of purpose Cal twisted and turned until the chair faced into the room. It was tiring and the sweat was soon running down his forehead.

He looked round slowly. There was little furniture. A bed with a grubby quilt thrown untidily over it. A chair with a book and a rush candle perched on top. Against the far wall was an oak chest, its heavy lid tight shut. Under the window there was a small writing desk with papers and writing materials strewn across it. There was nothing else.

Cal closed his eyes again but a rustling noise made them fly open and he strained to listen, his heart beating wildly. The sound was repeated. Only a mouse. Cal relaxed. Perhaps, he thought, he could get the mouse to gnaw at his bonds—he was sure he'd seen a movie where the hero escaped that way.

Yeah, but movies were one thing and life was another. He struggled again then slumped back on the chair. It was hopeless. He wasn't cut out to be a hero. Perhaps he'd better just sit tight and wait for Sturley's return. He sat still, watching the door. The rustling had stopped, but the house seemed full of noises, small furtive creaks as floorboards and furniture settled for the coming night. How long would it be before Sturley came?

Fear spread coldly from his stomach right through his body as Cal thought of the hard, round face, the thick lips, the cruel expression in the eyes. He was a big man, a strong man, Cal thought, remembering the grip of his arms as he had carried him up the stairs, a man who would enjoy violence, would enjoy hurting . . . and what could Cal tell him anyway? He would never believe the truth.

71

Cal began to rock the chair slowly towards the heavy wooden chest. If he could just lift the lid, there might be something inside which he could use to cut his bonds. He reached the chest and carefully rocked his chair around so that his back was close to it. His hands made contact with the wooden edge. He tried to lift it, but it was too heavy. His fingers explored the space between the lid and the box, feeling if there was a way of sliding his hand underneath. It was no use. The lid fitted tightly. Cal groaned in disappointment.

He looked again around the room. It was getting darker and the outlines of the objects were growing blurred. He looked at the bed, the chair, the writing desk . . . What was that feather doing, sticking upright out of some sort of pot? Cal dismissed it. A feather wasn't going to be much help in his escape. What he needed was a knife . . .

Didn't they write with feathers in those days? What was it they were called . . .? Quills, that was it. Quill pens. Memory flooded back. Himself, just a kid, running to his father with a large feather he had picked up in the garden. His father taking a knife and cutting the end to a fine point before sitting him down with a bottle of ink and some paper. He could remember laughing as he tried to write with the quill and ink sprayed out everywhere . . . Cal stiffened suddenly.

If they cut the ends of those feathers with a knife, there might just be a knife somewhere near that quill along with the jumble of stuff on the desk. It was worth a look.

He rocked his chair steadily across the room until he was in front of the desk. He examined its surface feverishly. Papers; books; something that looked like a half-written letter; the quill pen standing in an ink horn. Sturley must have been disturbed by the man in black in the middle of writing. And there, half hidden by the quill *was* a knife—a very small, very sharp knife. Cal stared at it for a long time.

72

All he had to do was get it off the desk, into his bound hands, and saw away at the ropes!

It would be a piece of cake to pick it up if only his hands were free! Cal let his head fall forwards on to the desk in despair.

Something wet and slightly sticky ran across his forehead. He lifted his head abruptly. A small stream of ink was running from the upset pot across the half-finished letter. It paused at the edge of the desk then began to drip slowly on to the floor. Cal stared at it, mesmerized.

He'll kill me when he gets back. The thought gave him a sickening jolt and he looked longingly at the knife on the far side of the desk.

Hey, wait a minute . . .

He dropped his head again to the desk and stretched his neck forwards as far as he could. The movement caused his wrists to hurt abominably but he scarcely noticed as he felt the brush of the quill touch his face. Just a little further, he thought, just a little . . . He took a breath, stretched his neck outwards and felt the edge of something hard against his forehead. Gotcha! Moving very gently he eased the knife sideways across the desk, lifting his head a number of times in order to check its progress, scarcely daring to breathe for fear that he would move it too far and it would fall to the floor. After what seemed an age, the knife lay balanced on the edge.

Cal rocked his chair around until he was at the side of the desk, his back to the knife. With painful slowness his fingers explored the edge and tightened thankfully around the sharp blade. Sweating with fear that he would drop it, Cal began sawing against the rope that bound his wrists together.

He nicked both his hands and his wrists, but scarcely noticed. At last one rope was cut through, then the other . . . and his hands were free! He dropped the knife and tried to tear off the gag but his hands refused to work. Frustrated, he rubbed his wrists and, with a rush of feeling, came

73

excruciating pain. He pulled off the gag, spitting the material out of his mouth, then untied his legs, fumbling at the knots with fingers that shook. He tried to stand, but his legs gave way under him and it was some minutes before he was able to stagger to the door. He lifted the latch. It was locked. Cal rattled it in a panic. His eyes blurred and his heart pounded.

Take a deep breath, he thought. Hey, cool down. He let go of the door and made himself look slowly round the room. It was now almost dark. He saw the pale outline of the window and went over to it. He kicked the pen-knife and absentmindedly picked it up and laid it on the writing desk, righting the horn of ink. He crumpled up the ruined half-written letter, and, with some vague thought about covering his traces, tried to open the drawer. It was locked. Cal suddenly remembered hearing the sound of a drawer being opened and shut and then he remembered the package that had been handed to Sturley by the man in black.

What was that package and what had become of it?

Cal seized the pen-knife and applied it to the desk drawer. The lock was weak and gave at the first pressure. He slid it open. It was too dark to see inside but he could feel something bulky. He picked it up and there was a faint rustle of paper. Quickly he stuffed the package inside his doublet then climbed on to the desk and wrenched open the small casement window. He stuck his head outside and looked down. It was too dark to see how far it was to the ground. He ran back to the door and tried his blade on the lock, but it was far stronger than that of the desk and would not yield. He returned to the window and tried to think. The upper storey of the inn overhung the lower and he remembered having to duck his head in order to peer in at the lower window. In that case it could not be too great a drop to the steps outside. Anyway, he would have to risk it.

He climbed out of the window, held on to the lower sill with his hands and felt with his feet. Nothing. Closing his eyes and trying to relax his body, he let go and dropped . . . straight into the arms of someone waiting below. A hand gripped his wrist and twisted it painfully behind his back.

Sweat broke out on his forehead and he felt cold and sick. The night rushed over him and he could see nothing . . .

. . . except the sun-drenched pavement on London Bridge. The hand on his wrist tightened for a moment and then let go.

'As ever, Cal, you are late. The coach nearly went without you.'

Cal looked up into John Loveday's face. It showed nothing except mild annoyance. 'Get on, can't you, don't just stand there.'

Cal turned and mounted the steps and his entry was greeted by jeers and catcalls. Silently, he made for a vacant seat. John followed him and took the seat across the aisle. The door swung shut and the coach moved off.

Cal's hand crept to his shirt and he patted it gently. There, safe inside and close to his chest, was the feel of a bulky package and the faint rustle of paper. Whatever it was, Cal had brought it back with him. Back into the twentieth century.

Chapter Seven

The journey to Stratford seemed never-ending. The group was tired and subdued and most of them were soon asleep, but Cal, although weary to the point of exhaustion, remained wide awake, questions chasing one another around his tired brain.

Who was the stranger who had caught him as he jumped from the window? From time to time he glanced at John, who appeared to be sleeping. Was it only coincidence that John had been holding his wrist when Cal returned to the present, or was John Loveday somehow involved? Then what about Philip Sturley? What part did he play in all this? And above all, what *was* in the package? If it was in fact the missing manuscript what on earth should he do with it? Somehow he had to get it back, for it belonged to Shakespeare and not to the present.

It was all so complicated. Cal stirred uncomfortably in his seat, feeling that in some way he had acted like a fool. He settled himself to sleep, but his mind was racing so he opened his eyes and looked out at the dark blur of the countryside as the coach sped along the motorway. He leaned his forehead against the window and it felt cold to the touch. What should he tell Hamnet, Susanna, and Judith, always supposing that he did return to the past? If he *was* able to take the manuscript back with him then his task was over. If not . . .

That brought him once more to the question that had been at the back of his mind ever since the whole thing had begun. Why him? Why not Nicky, say, who was born and brought up in Stratford, with roots that probably stretched back generations? Why him, a stranger? Perhaps, he thought, hovering on the edge of sleep, that might be the reason. He was chosen because he *was* a stranger, uninvolved and unbiased—not that he was either now.

Cal's last thought before he slept was to remind himself to read up the part of Moth in *A Midsummer Night's Dream*. If he did return to the past as one of Shakespeare's players, he wouldn't want to go through another rehearsal like the last one. Neither would he want to let Shakespeare down. Cal slept . . .

He jerked awake as they turned off the M40, and he remained awake and alert as the coach drove the short distance to Stratford and pulled up outside their guest house. No one wanted to stay up late and Cal, after getting himself a drink from the kitchen, was the last up the stairs. The bedroom was in darkness.

'You're not going to turn the light on are you?' grumbled a sleepy voice from under a mass of duvet.

'That's okay,' Cal replied. 'I'll undress in the dark.'

There was a grunt then the sound of slow, measured breathing. Cal waited a few minutes before tiptoeing quietly out of the room. He crossed the landing, went into the bathroom and locked the door. He turned on the light. His heart was beating in great heavy thumps and his throat felt tight with excitement. He sat on the lavatory and took out the package.

It was wrapped in some kind of lightly-oiled skin and tied with thin cord. Cal untied it with trembling fingers, removed the outer covering, and a mass of tightly folded sheets of paper were revealed. They were yellow with age and the paper was stiff and crackly. Cal was afraid they might crumble away, but they unfolded under his careful touch into large sheets of paper. Each page was covered with thin, spidery, black writing. Cal bent his head but it was impossible to make out any words. It could have been written in a different language for all the sense he could make of it. Then he caught sight of the heading at the top of the first page.

Love's Labour's Won,
a play by William Shakespeare

Cal caught his breath with excitement. It was, it surely was, the missing manuscript. Reverently he laid out the pages across the floor of the bathroom and stared at them. Boy, if what John Loveday said was true, these sheets of paper were worth a fortune and collectors throughout the world would be cutting each other's throats to get hold of them.

Cutting each other's throats and cutting his if they got the chance. Murder would be nothing to what would happen if anyone got wind of what was in front of him. He remembered the obsessive look on John Loveday's face when Cal had asked about *Love's Labour's Won* and heard his voice, the voice of a fanatic: 'I'd give ten years of my life—no, more—if I could find something like this.' Quickly Cal began to collect up the sheets. It was not his job to sell to the highest bidder. No way. His task was somehow to return it safely where it belonged.

Someone was knocking on the bathroom door. Hurriedly Cal folded the manuscript into its wrapping and retied the cord.

'Hold on!'

'Say, you gonna be in there all night?'

'Nearly ready.'

He stuffed the manuscript back into his shirt, remembered to flush the lavatory and unlocked the door.

It was Carole.

'I thought you'd died in there or something.'

'No. I'm okay.'

'But you're not even undressed for God's sake!'

'Yeah—I mean no—I didn't feel so good. Must be something I ate,' Cal muttered, edging past her.

She stared after him as he bolted across the landing and into his own room. Quickly he threw off his clothes and burrowed into bed, the manuscript safe under his pillow. But sleep eluded him.

What should he do with it? If it was so valuable, perhaps he ought to give it to someone for safe-keeping? But who could he trust? Suddenly, with a sense of longing that was like a sharp pain, he thought of his father. He could trust his father. His father would know what to do. Quickly he turned his thoughts elsewhere. John Loveday? No. Who then?

Cal thought harder. Hold on a minute. He could not give the manuscript to anyone. He had to keep it close about him, otherwise how could it be returned to the past? It had to stay with him so that it could travel back in time, if, and when, he did.

Relieved at having solved one problem Cal turned over and settled himself for sleep. But just as he was drifting off he had another thought. A thought that made him sit bolt upright. Nicky—what was her part in all this? How was it that she always managed to turn up, knowing exactly where and when to find him? There was something odd about it. He thought of Nicky and her round open face and grinned. He'd be getting a complex about all this if he wasn't careful, and start suspecting Carole or Lou or Greg or the rest of the gang . . . He snuggled down in bed, pulled the duvet over his head and fell fast asleep.

But the following morning he was not altogether surprised when Nicky hailed him as he came out of Waterstones Bookshop, a paperback copy of *A Midsummer Night's Dream* rather self-consciously in his hand.

'Hi.'

'Hi.'

They walked along together.

'How was London?'

'Great—terrific.'

'Really?' Nicky wrinkled up her nose. 'I've been there loads of times, of course, but I don't reckon it much. Too noisy, too dirty, and too crowded.'

She turned to more important things. 'Anything happened?'

Cal was silent for a moment.

'In what way . . .?' he began at last.

Nicky glanced at him. 'You don't trust me do you?'

'What do you mean?'

'Oh, come on,' she said impatiently. '*Something* happened, that's obvious, it sticks out a mile, but for some reason you don't want to tell me. Why?'

Cal was silent.

'I'm your *friend*,' she said. 'I'm on *your* side. I'm positively green with envy about you leaping off into the past and not me, but I'll help if I can.'

They pushed their way past the people on the pavement and Cal's fears vanished. It was all so normal. A warm August day rooted in the present. Impossible to suspect Nicky of goodness knows what. Impossible, in some ways, to believe in the terror he had felt with the edge of the dagger pricking at his throat and the tightness of the ropes that had bound him. But yet, that had all been real. Cal had the marks at his ankles and wrists as proof.

He hesitated for a moment, then began to speak. She listened eagerly, stopping him from time to time with questions. He told her about the events at The Theatre and did not gloss over his own stupidity in following Philip.

'You'd have done it a whole heap better,' he admitted humbly.

'Maybe. But go on, what did he do?'

So Cal went on with the story of his capture and escape.

'And then I had the darnedest luck,' he said. 'I dropped right out of the window and straight into the arms of . . .'

They had reached the crossroads and paused there, oblivious of the crowds jostling round them.

'Who?'

'I don't know,' Cal said slowly. 'I came back into the present.'

'Oh, that's not fair!'

Cal grinned wryly. 'I don't know about that. I was quite glad to find it was only "The Stiff" gripping my wrist.'

'And the manuscript . . .?'

'I've got it,' he said slowly.

Nicky's eyes were alight with excitement. 'You've got it? Here?'

Cal nodded his head.

'But . . . where?'

Cal patted the holdall he was carrying. 'I can't leave it around anywhere. It could get stolen or thrown away. Anyway, if I don't have it with me I can't take it back into the past.'

'Can I—can I *see* it?' Nicky asked in a breathless voice.

'Well . . .' Cal looked down at her flushed, excited face. 'Okay. But not here. It's too public.'

They went down to the river and crossed the bridge to the small island in the centre. It was quite deserted.

Cal took out the manuscript and unfolded it carefully, keeping tight hold of the pages in the slight breeze. He laughed at Nicky's disappointed face.

'It's in a foreign language.'

'I thought so at first, but it's not. Look.' He traced the title. '*Love's Labour's Won.*'

Nicky stared at it, wrinkling her nose in concentration.

'Why's the paper so crumbly?'

'I guess because it's four hundred years old. You'd be a bit crumbly if you were that age.'

'Was it like that when you got it?'

Cal began to fold up the sheets. 'I don't know. I didn't have time to look. But I guess not. I guess it must have gotten that way as I carried it through time.'

He retied the cord and placed the package in his holdall.

'What are you going to do with it?'

Cal shrugged. 'Not much I can do except keep it safe and hope I go back some time to return it.'

'Can't you *make* yourself go back?'

'I tried, but I can't. It doesn't seem to work like that. It's not anything I can control. Maybe if I was older or understood more about it . . .'

There was a faint sound behind them. Cal whipped round but the path behind him was deserted. He looked suspiciously at the bushes and trees surrounding the bank on which they were sitting, but there was no sign of anyone. He shrugged.

'I'm getting the jitters.' He got to his feet. 'Anyway, I got to go. Promised the gang I'd go for a bathe.'

'Can I come?'

'Nope.' Her face fell at his decided voice.

'Look, don't hustle me, Nicky. I'm worried enough as it is. It's no joke carrying this thing around. I feel like I've got those crown jewels of yours burning a hole in my pocket.'

'Not my crown jewels,' she said.

'You know what I mean.'

'Okay,' she said, disappointed. 'See you around.'

'Yeah. See you.'

He ran off down the path and crossed the bridge. Nicky followed more slowly. A lightly sarcastic voice spoke from behind her.

'Aren't you rather young to be having secret assignations, sister dear? I'll have to tell mother to keep her eye on you when I'm back at college.'

Cal poised for a moment on the edge of the deep end, then dived in. Gene followed, and they raced each other down the length of the baths. Cal swam strongly but Gene soon overtook him and won comfortably.

Cal turned on his back and floated. The water felt good. Some of the tensions of the past few days drained away. He was glad now that he had been persuaded to go in the water, for when they had arrived at the Leisure Centre he had had a sudden moment of panic. What would he do with the manuscript? He could not very well take it into the pool.

'Uh, I think I'll sit this out,' he said uncomfortably once they had reached the changing room.

Gene, busy undressing, stopped and looked at him. 'You crazy or something? You bring your gear, pay your money, get to the changing room and now you say you'll sit it out?'

'Well . . .' Cal shrugged.

'C'mon, don't be such a jerk. You afraid of catching something? Say, guys,' he called across to Franklin and Greg, 'this dumb jerk thinks he'll catch something from the pool!'

'No, I don't . . .'

Between them they had shamed Cal into changing into his swimming trunks. He stowed the manuscript deep into his holdall and locked it firmly in one of the lockers. The key, attached to a large silver safety pin, was secured to his swimming trunks.

'Glad you came in?' Greg shouted across at him.

'Yeah. Great.'

'C'mon then, race you down the other end.'

They set off at a fast crawl but their race ended in a tangle of arms and legs when Lou and Carole jumped in on top of them. Carole shook her wet hair from her eyes and looked up.

'Hey, d'you see who's there?' She began to wave towards the glass-fronted refreshment room, which ran on a higher level down one side of the swimming pool.

'Coo-ee . . .!'

'They won't hear you.'

'Look! It's "The Stiff".'

Cal jerked his head round and stared upwards. It was indeed 'The Stiff'. He was sitting with someone, looking down into the pool.

Carole screwed up her eyes. 'Hey, guys, guess who's with him . . . it's that gorgeous actor we met the other day. Richard thingummy.' She waved more vigorously. 'Come on in, handsome,' she called, 'it's great in here!'

Gene pulled her under the water. 'Don't make such an ass of yourself! They'll chuck us out!'

'He's left the table,' said Franklin, gazing up. 'Perhaps he *is* coming to join us.'

It was true. As Cal watched, Richard Wantage stood up and left the restaurant. Cal swam away from the group. He did not want company right now. He wanted to think.

The shouts from the swimmers grew distant. The water was warm and felt silky soft against his skin. He swam a few lengths then turned on his back and floated once more, half-closing his eyes . . .

His mouth and nose filled with water as he was dragged under. The shock of it made him thrash around wildly, but his legs were held in a strong grip. He tried to shout—'Hey cut it out!'—but the words were inside his head. The pain in his chest was excruciating. His lungs were bursting. The tiles on the sides and floor of the pool danced, dipping and swaying at crazy angles, magnified in the clear green water. There was thudding in his ears and his head was cracking open with the pressure. 'Let me breathe, Oh God, let me breathe!' The green of the water exploded in brilliant flashes of light and the colours stabbed through his head until he could not bear the pain any more . . . and then everything went black . . .

. . . there were shifting patterns in the darkness—sunlight slanting on the water . . . and a hand held down to clutch at his and pull him strongly out of the swift-flowing current, out of the reeds that clung around his legs, and out of the river. He was landed like a wet fish, gasping and wriggling.

'I told you the river could be treacherous.'

Hamnet watched Cal coughing and retching on the bank.

84

'Tha's—okay. I'm . . . okay . . .now . . .'

'The current is swift-flowing.'

'Yeah . . .'

Cal leant over the water's edge and was violently sick.

'That's better.' He sat up gingerly and began to shiver. He looked down at himself. No wonder he was cold, he was completely naked.

'Is there aught I can do?' Hamnet asked, worried.

'I'm okay . . . just, just cold,' Cal said through teeth that were beginning to chatter.

Hamnet raced across the bank and flung him a bundle of clothes. 'Here! I know the river well, but it's dangerous. Father doesn't like me to swim here, but . . .' he shrugged. 'He used to swim here himself so he doesn't scold too hard.'

By this time Cal had struggled into his shirt and hose, feeling the material stick uncomfortably to his wet skin. He got to his feet and staggered slightly.

'Wait.' Hamnet was by his side. 'Lean on me.'

'I'm okay, honest.' Cal straightened up. He took a deep, steadying breath. 'Thanks.'

'It was naught.'

'Well, you sure were there when I needed you,' Cal said feelingly.

'I'm glad.' Hamnet smiled in relief. 'Come. Supper is ready and mother will be waiting for us.'

'Just a minute.' Cal put out his hand. 'There's something I've got to tell you.' He paused for a moment, not quite knowing where to begin. 'I've found the manuscript.'

Hamnet's face lit up. 'You've found it? Where?'

'It's a bit of a long story,' Cal said slowly. He shivered suddenly. 'Look, can't we sit down? I guess I can't walk and talk at the same time.'

They sat on the bank and Cal recounted his story for the second time.

'And this man Sturley is a player with father's company?' Hamnet interrupted.

'Yeah. Well, he's hired in, I reckon. There was something about another actor being sick.'

'Father should know of his treachery.'

'How can you tell him without explaining about the manuscript?'

Hamnet bit his lip.

'Besides, who was the other man, the one I saw in the inn, the man in black? He gave Sturley the manuscript so I guess he's the one who stole it in the first place.'

'Aye.' Hamnet was silent for a moment then said resolutely, 'I think I should tell father.'

'No. Wait. You haven't heard it all.'

Cal continued with the story of his imprisonment and escape. Hamnet stared at him, open mouthed.

'So you have the manuscript?' Hamnet asked when Cal had finished. 'You took it away with you?'

'Yeah.'

'Where is it?'

'Well, like I said . . .' Cal felt uncomfortable. 'I returned to my own time . . .'

'But you're here now. You brought it with you?'

'No, I couldn't . . .'

'But why?'

Cal was tired. 'Well, dammit, you hauled me out of the river! I didn't have a stitch of clothing on me let alone a priceless manuscript!'

'So where is it?' Hamnet was on his feet, shaking Cal's arm.

'Hey, let go of me! I'm trying to remember!'

'I beg pardon.' Hamnet sat down once more.

'Don't you think *I* feel bad about it?' Cal asked.

They sat in silence while Cal tried to think. But his brain felt sluggish and the harder he tried, the more difficult it became.

'I was going somewhere but I can't remember . . .' he said at last. 'There was something about water, the river . . .

no, it wasn't the river—there were tiles floating towards me
...oh gee...'

'Perhaps it fell into the river,' Hamnet said despondently.

Cal frowned with the effort of concentration.

'No. I guess I put it safe . . .' his voice trailed off uncertainly. 'I'm *sure* I put it safe. Oh, *why* can't I remember?' He thumped the ground with his fists in frustration, then looked at Hamnet. 'I'm sorry. But I'll find it. I promise. I'll get it back to you somehow.'

Chapter Eight

The evening meal, taken round the large oak table in Shakespeare's home, was a noisy affair. Cal sat at the far end wedged between Hamnet and Susanna, and wondered what would happen if he were noticed by their mother. But his presence seemed to be taken for granted. One more mouth to feed in the large household was neither here nor there for Mistress Anne Shakespeare. She was a plump, homely lady, placid and unruffled, and her likeness to her elder daughter was marked.

Cal relaxed a little. The room was warm and seemed to be full of people. Shakespeare was not there but Hamnet obligingly pointed out his other relations in between hungry bites of bread and cheese.

'There's grandfather,' he said, waving his knife in the direction of a big, grey-haired man at the head of the table. 'He owns the glove-making shop next door—and that's grandmother beside him.' Cal obediently looked at them but his attention was caught by a smiling, attractive lady who was seated on one of the benches, talking animatedly to a serious-looking man beside her.

'That's Aunt Joan with Master Hart,' Hamnet said in his ear. 'He's a hatter and has been courting Aunt for ages. They haven't yet called the banns for the wedding but Susanna says they will marry this year and she usually knows.' He took a mouthful of food and his gaze travelled on round the table. 'That's Uncle Edmund—he's sixteen and wants to be a player like father, but father doesn't want him.'

'Why?' Cal asked.

Hamnet grinned. 'Father *says* it's too hard a life but I think the real reason is that Uncle Edmund has but small talent.' He laughed. 'That's Uncle Richard next to him, and beside *him* is Uncle Gilbert. He lives with us when he's in Stratford but he works in London at a haberdasher's.'

'Who are the rest?'

Hamnet shrugged. 'Oh, they're just the journeymen and apprentices from grandfather's shop. They eat with us and some of them sleep in the attic next door.'

The room was warm, for despite the mild summer evening a fire burned brightly under a large cooking pot. Cal, dry now and well fed on the simple meal of bread, cold meat, and cheese, began to grow sleepy. At the top end of the table, Hamnet's grandfather was speaking, but Cal paid little attention. He looked around. The ceiling was low and crossed with dark wooden beams while the floor was strewn with fresh straw. There was little furniture in the room other than the table at which they sat, a high-backed carved chair, a large chest, and a dresser, but everything was well polished and smelt of beeswax.

The door opened softly and Judith entered the room. She hurried to her place at the table.

'I'm sorry I'm late, mother. The chickens . . . '

The rest of her apology was lost as she sank on to the bench and bent her head. Her lips were pressed tightly together and there were two spots of colour on her cheeks. Her eyes were puffy and swollen and Cal thought she had been crying. Her grandfather glanced at her sharply.

'Now then, child, what's amiss?'

'Nothing, grandfather.'

She put some food on her plate, but made no real attempt to eat. Her grandfather stared at her and was about to speak again when there was a stir from outside. The door was flung open and Shakespeare came striding in, bringing a breath of evening air into the stuffy, over-warm room.

'Forgive me, Anne, for arriving at this hour and with no warning. We were meant to be at Coventry, but the costumes went astray and Philip and I have been hunting all over the county for them.'

Anne got to her feet. 'And you found them?'

'Aye, eventually, in Warwick. The carter had delivered them to the wrong Bell Inn! Being so near, I thought to come home for the night and beg a bed for Philip here.' He beckoned to the man who was hovering in the doorway. 'Come in, Philip.' He turned back to his wife. 'Anne, my love, allow me to present Master Sturley, who has nobly stepped in to Will Kempe's part during his sickness. Philip, my wife, Anne.'

Philip swept a bow. 'Mistress, the honour is mine.'

Anne curtsied then glanced at her husband. 'You must both be tired and hungry.'

'Not so tired, but ravenously hungry, although we deserve nothing coming so late and unexpected.'

Anne smiled. Servants were sent scurrying to lay fresh trenchers and food and the apprentices and journeymen were banished to their part of the house. Cal retreated to a dark corner and watched Philip Sturley.

Shakespeare threw himself into his big carved chair with a contented sigh and seated Sturley beside him. Hamnet, after a brief questioning glance at Cal, poured tankards of ale and took them to his father. Shakespeare smiled and ruffled Hamnet's hair.

'Let me introduce you to our guest. My son Hamnet.'

Hamnet bowed and Shakespeare looked round. 'Where is Susanna?' he asked. 'I would have Master Sturley know what a fine family I have.'

'Here, father.' Susanna curtsied.

'My eldest daughter,' Shakespeare said proudly.

He took a long drink of ale.

'Oh, that is good.' He stretched himself and turned to his guest. 'Now then, Philip, if you would return to the inn tomorrow to watch over the costumes . . .'

'I too am here, sir.' A small, precise voice interrupted from the corner of the room and Judith came stiffly into the light.

Shakespeare turned to her. 'Judith, my child. Forgive me, I'm tired. Philip, my other daughter.'

Judith gave a small, dignified curtsy.

'Now, be off with you, children. All of you. Master Sturley and I have matters to discuss.'

'Come,' said Hamnet and Cal followed him outside.

'You don't mind sleeping in the barn do you?' Hamnet asked as they crossed the garden.

'Okay by me.'

'As you see, our house is already overflowing, and with the guest father brought home . . . '

They went into the barn and Hamnet led the way up a narrow ladder.

'This Master Sturley, is he the same man you were telling me about?' Hamnet asked.

'Yeah.'

'And father brought him here . . . ?'

'Just coincidence, I guess.'

'Maybe.'

The loft was large and filled with straw. Hamnet pulled some of it into a corner and made a nest.

'It's clean and sweet-smelling. You'll be comfortable here.'

'Oh sure.'

'There's no danger to father?' Hamnet asked thoughtfully.

Cal was silent for a moment, then shook his head. 'I guess not. I can't see how.'

Hamnet nodded and went over to the ladder. 'Goodnight then, Cal. We can talk with my sisters tomorrow.'

'Goodnight.'

And Hamnet was gone, taking the stub of the candle with him. Cal went over to the low, unglazed window, knelt

91

down, and looked into the garden. Cool night air flowed across his face. The garden was lit only fitfully by a pale moon and seemed filled with shadows. Cal's skin prickled with apprehension.

Perhaps Sturley had not seen him? The room had been dimly lit and Cal had kept well back into the shadows. But then he remembered the swift encompassing glance Sturley had cast around the room as he had entered and the faint look of surprise, quickly suppressed, as his gaze had swept past Cal. He had been seen, all right—and recognized.

Perhaps he should leave the barn and find some other place in which to spend the night? But where? He felt safer somehow within the stout walls, less exposed than he would out in the garden. Besides, Sturley was unlikely to know that he had been housed there, and he would be unable to search the house for fear of waking someone. Cal stared across the grass. A dim light was still showing in the lower room but, as he watched, it was extinguished. Surely Shakespeare would not leave his guest until he had seen him comfortably settled for the night? Cal watched and waited, his eyes fixed on the house and garden, but there was no movement.

An owl hooted and the wind began to freshen. Cal felt cold and cramped. He stood up and stamped his feet. With one last look outside he left the window and went to his nest in the straw, pulling it over and around him in thick piles. It tickled and he sneezed, the noise sounding over-loud in the quiet barn. Perhaps, he thought, he'd stay awake a bit, just to make sure . . .

He woke some hours later to feel a hand clamped over his mouth and the cold, familiar sensation of a dagger at his neck.

'One squeal and you're dead,' said a quiet voice close to his ear.

Cal lay silent. The hand slowly withdrew.

'You won't get away so easily this time, little Moth. Not unless you can fly.'

Footsteps moved across the loft. A light was struck and a candle lit. It was quickly shaded and placed in a dark corner, away from the opening.

Philip Sturley, a black figure silhouetted in the candle's soft glow, turned to Cal.

'Now then, lad,' he said pleasantly. 'Just give me the package and I'll leave you to a sweet night's sleep.' He held out his hand.

'What package?' Cal asked. The hand struck him hard across the mouth.

'The package you stole from my room. Come, the time for jest is over!'

'I don't have it,' Cal said nervously. Sturley struck him again. 'That for your lies! Now, where is it!'

'I—I haven't got it . . . honest.'

Sturley's face grew hard. 'You dare lie to me! You stole it from my desk!' He grabbed Cal's arm. 'Get up!' He hauled Cal to his feet, ripped off his doublet and shirt, then threw him to one side. Seizing the candle and holding it high, he pulled the straw, which had formed Cal's bed, to pieces. Cal watched, too winded and too frightened to make a move. Sturley prowled round the loft, poking into every corner and kicking the straw around viciously before rounding on Cal, dagger in his hand.

'I have been too gentle with you, boy,' he said with quiet menace. 'Tell me where you have hid it or by heaven I'll give you a taste of this.'

He approached Cal slowly.

'I don't have it! I keep telling you!'

He grabbed Cal's arm and forced him on to his knees.

'Then where is it!' he demanded. 'Who have you given it to?'

'No one!'

93

'You try my patience.' His grip on Cal's arm tightened. 'Where is the package?'

'It isn't here!'

Sturley stared down at him. 'Very well,' he said at last. 'You will take me to it. Now.'

'I—I can't . . . ' Sturley struck him and the blow sent Cal reeling back against the wall.

'I *can't*!'

'Speak plainly, boy, for your life depends on it. Why cannot you take me to where you have hid the package?'

Cal swallowed. 'Because . . . '

'Well?' Sturley was towering over him.

'Because it's in the future,' Cal said desperately. 'Four hundred years away. I took it into my own time!'

There was silence. Sturley stared at Cal. His hand went up as if to ward off evil, then his expression hardened and his eyes became menacing slits in his round face.

'You lying little fool . . . '

He seized Cal by the hair, forcing his head backwards. He raised his other hand. The dagger glinted.

'No! No! Please! Wait . . . ' Cal struggled, trying to move out of the range of the dagger that was flashing downwards, silver in the moonlight . . . that was a star blazing through the night sky, bursting over and inside Cal's head in an explosion of light, dazzling his eyes, blinding him with its intensity, searing into his brain with its white-hot fire . . .

. . . and through the pain he could hear Sturley's voice, no longer menacing now but full of fear.

'Sweet Lord preserve us! He vanishes before my eyes!'

Then everything went black.

'All right, now, just take it easy now, take it easy.'

The firm hands pressing down on the small of his back shifted as Cal moved his head.

'Don't try to move. Just relax.'

Cal opened his eyes and found himself staring at a concrete floor. He closed his eyes again. He was wet and shivering and suddenly knew he was going to be sick. He moved involuntarily and felt himself being lifted gently.

'All right?'

'I—feel sick . . .'

'I'm not surprised.'

One hand supported his back, while the other pressed his head down towards his knees. Cal struggled for a moment, then relaxed. The sickness passed. Cautiously he opened his eyes. He could see the swimming pool, a vast expanse of greenish-blue water. Memory began to return. The pressure of the hand on his head was removed.

'Feeling better now?'

He looked up into the concerned face of a pool attendant. Beside her stood Gene, Carole, Greg, Franklin, and Lou, their faces white and anxious.

'I—I'm okay.'

'You must have blacked out for a moment,' the girl said. 'The first thing we knew was when someone shouted. You were lying face down in the water.'

'Yeah?' There was something wrong, something that did not make sense but Cal felt too weary to worry about it. His head was thumping too much.

'Would you like a cup of tea? You're still a bit groggy.'

'No—I . . . ' Cal struggled to his feet. Willing hands came to his aid. He looked down at his legs, a bit astonished to find them working. Then full memory returned.

'My key. It's gone!'

'What key?' The girl was patient.

'The key to the locker!' Cal could feel himself shaking. 'It was pinned to my trunks!'

'It's all right. I've got a master key.'

'That's not the point . . . !' he shouted.

Greg pushed himself forwards. 'Is this what you're looking for?' he asked, holding out a key attached to a safety pin. 'Found it at the bottom of the pool after they brought you out. You couldn't have pinned it on properly.'

95

Cal nodded. 'Yeah, that's it. Thanks,' He shook off the restraining hands. 'I—I think I'd like to change if that's okay.' He shivered and pulled the towel closer round him. 'I'm a bit cold . . . '

'Of course. Would you like me to come with you?'

'No. I'm okay. Honest.'

'We'll look after him,' said Gene, taking his arm.

Cal slowly made his way towards the changing room, flanked by Gene, Greg, and Franklin. Once inside, he turned on them.

'Did one of you play that trick and pull me under?' he asked bluntly.

All three looked surprised. 'We weren't anywhere near you,' Gene said.

'You'd gone off by yourself down the other end,' Greg added.

'You saying that someone tried to drown you?' Franklin asked incredulously.

'Yeah.'

Gene shrugged. 'Perhaps it was some kid. There were loads messing around.' He looked at Cal with concern. 'Give me your key and I'll get your grip. You're still shaking.'

'I'm okay.'

Cal shook them off and went over to his locker. With trembling fingers he slipped the key into the lock and opened the door. His holdall was where he had placed it, thrust deep inside. He drew it out and took it over to a bench. The others were watching him. Cal glanced up and managed to grin.

'I'm okay, guys. Takes more than a ducking to get rid of me.'

Reassured, the others turned away.

What else does it take to get rid of me, Cal thought grimly as he stared at his holdall. He had already been twice near drowned, attacked with a knife, and beaten up.

The side of his face was still stinging and his arm and side felt bruised where Sturley had thrown him against the wall.

He unzipped the bag, placed his hands inside and carefully removed the contents, one after another. There was no manuscript. Of course not. He had known it from the moment he had realized that the key had gone.

Someone had dragged him under water, unpinned the key from his trunks, possibly raised the alarm and, under cover of the commotion, slipped into the changing room, taken his holdall from the locker and removed the manuscript. Then he—or she—had replaced the holdall and tossed the key into the pool.

Cal sat on the bench and tried to think. Who had known about the manuscript? Only one person. Nicky. He had to find Nicky.

It was difficult shaking off the gang. They insisted on taking him up to the restaurant and buying him tea. He looked round, but Loveday and Wantage had gone.

'Say, did that actor-guy have a bathe in the end?'

'Nope, he didn't show up,' said Carole regretfully. 'And I thought he fancied me.'

'He did show up,' said Lou unexpectedly. 'He dived in the deep end—near where you were,' she said to Cal. 'I didn't see him after that because there was all that fuss over you.'

'Perhaps it was *Cal* he fancied and not Carole,' said Greg grinning maliciously. 'Maybe he was the one who pulled Cal under.'

'Funny way to show you fancy someone,' Carole replied tartly.

The others laughed, but Cal sat sipping his tea thoughtfully. Had Wantage dragged him under? Wantage, who had been sitting in the restaurant with Loveday only minutes before. Wantage and Loveday? And Nicky?

He managed to get away from the others outside the Leisure Centre.

97

'Leave me alone a bit, okay? I just want some fresh air.'

'Don't go falling into the river,' joked Greg, and they went off, back to the guest house.

Nicky hailed him a minute later, detaching herself from behind a parked car.

'I was waiting for you,' she said simply, then stopped and stared.

'You all right? Your face is all puffy.'

'So would yours be if you'd been beaten up and then half-drowned.'

Her eyes widened. 'What?'

He told her briefly. When he had finished there was silence.

'So the manuscript has gone . . . ?' she said blankly.

'Yep.'

'Who on earth could have taken it?'

'That's what I want to know,' Cal said deliberately. 'Who knew about the manuscript? I've only told one person.'

Her face began to turn red. 'You don't think . . . ' she began hotly.

'I don't know what to think. You tell me.'

'Look . . . !' She stopped suddenly and bit her lip.

'Look what? You look. The only person I've told is you, so I think you've got a bit of explaining to do, don't you? Like how someone, if it wasn't you, knew that the manuscript would be in my grip and near-drowned me to get hold of it? Like what's your tie-up with Loveday and Wantage? Like how come you always know where to find me? Stratford's not a big place, but it's big enough.'

Nicky was silent.

They had been walking towards the town and crossed the Clopton Bridge at the bottom of Bridge Street. Nicky made a sudden move, but Cal grabbed her arm.

'You're not going till I get some answers!'

'You beast!'

He held on to her and led her to a wall overlooking the canal. She glanced at him once or twice but did not speak until they were sitting side by side. Then she laughed.

'Okay, boss, I'll come clean.' She took a deep breath. 'He's my brother.'

'What?'

'John's my brother.'

'John . . . ?' Cal stared at her. 'You mean that *Loveday* is your *brother*?'

'Yep.' She wriggled her feet. 'But if you think he's got anything to do with it you're wrong. He isn't like that.'

'So that's how you always knew where I could be found?' Cal said slowly.

Nicky nodded. 'It was great. You always looked so surprised when I turned up and I didn't see why you should have all the fun.'

'Did you *tell* him?' Cal asked sharply.

'You never said it was a secret,' Nicky said defensively.

'No—I guess I never thought—but *why* did you tell him?'

'I thought I could find things out for you. I asked him about that play and then he asked *me* why I wanted to know.'

'So you told him?'

'Yes.'

'And what did he say?'

'He said it was a load of rubbish, you going back into the past. He said you could have made it all up, all that about Shakespeare, because your father teaches history at a university in America and he could have told you about it. But I know you didn't make it up. So I told him I'd really *seen* the manuscript . . .'

'You told him that?'

'Yes.'

'When?'

'Just after you showed it to me.'

99

Cal was thoughtful. 'That rustling noise. He must've been snooping round.'

'He wasn't snooping!'

'Look, Nicky,' Cal said wearily. 'Do you know what you've done? That manuscript, which doesn't belong to me or to your precious brother, has been stolen by him, or maybe by Wantage who's probably his partner, and until I can get it back there's no way I can return it to Hamnet.'

Nicky turned bright red. 'He *couldn't* have stolen it. He didn't believe me! He said he didn't!'

'He was just stringing you along,' Cal said cynically. 'Of course he believed you and now he's got the manuscript and half-drowned me in the process.'

'But he wouldn't do a thing like that! He wouldn't! Anyway *why* would he want it?'

'It's worth a lot of money.'

'John doesn't care about money! He's a . . . a scholar,' she said with dignity.

'Okay, but he'd want it all right,' Cal said. 'He's a nutter about things like that. He told me.'

'He's not! He's *not*! And I think you're mean and beastly and hateful and I wish I'd never met you!'

Choking back a sob, she jumped down from the wall and ran off up Bridge Street.

Cal started after her. 'Wait! Hey, Nicky, wait!'

The street lurched drunkenly towards him. The houses began to topple and fall forwards and Cal cushioned his head in his arms instinctively for protection. But there was no sound of falling masonry and no feeling under his feet of the earthquake that was engulfing him.

Cautiously he lifted his head and saw the retreating figure of Judith hurrying away between the leafy elm trees of Fore Bridge Street.

Chapter Nine

Despite the presence of forty boys, the large schoolroom was fairly peaceful. In one corner, a group of the youngest were struggling with Latin, reciting out loud as an usher listened and corrected. In another corner, some nine year olds were learning how to make quill pens under the watchful eye of a senior pupil, while a third group were busily spattering themselves and each other with ink as they stood behind high wooden desks practising writing.

The centre of the room was presided over by the Master, a tall, thin-faced man, who sat on a raised stand like some black, brooding bird. In front of him, the eleven and twelve year olds were seated on long wooden benches. Their chanting voices, quoting by heart from Lily's Grammar, mingled with the Latin verbs and nouns of the younger boys. The recitation came to an end and the Master left his seat and stepped down from the dais. He began to walk slowly up and down among the benches.

'Fulke, *"Tibi parata sunt verba, huic verbera"*, *dixit Terentius noster. Ultrum vis,* Fulke?' ('Fulke. "Words have been prepared for you, blows for this man," said Terence. Which of the two do you want, Fulke?')

'*Verba, Magister.*' ('Words, Master.')

'*Sapiens es,* Fulke.' ('You are wise, Fulke.')

Sunlight floated in through the windows, throwing diamond-shaped lozenges of light on to the dark oak desks, the scrubbed wooden floor, and the bare heads of the pupils. Hamnet, lulled almost to sleep by the chanting voices, watched the sun playing on the motes of dust that hung suspended in the air and wondered what had become of Cal.

A shadow cut off the light and a ferula descended on to his shoulder. Hamnet jerked abruptly awake.

'Hamnet, *fur diviti insidias conlocat. Uter alterum minatur?*' ('Hamnet, a thief is laying an ambush for a rich man. Which one is threatening the other?')

'*Dives furem minatur,*' ('The rich man is threatening the thief,') Hamnet replied without thinking.

'*Stultus es*, Hamnet,' ('You are foolish, Hamnet,') the Master said in a weary voice.

'I beg pardon, sir,' Hamnet said confusedly.

There was a rustling and murmuring among the other pupils. It was forbidden to speak anything other than Latin during school hours.

'*Surge.*'

Hamnet stood.

'*Tende manum.*'

Hamnet held out his hand, palm uppermost, and the ferula came down forcefully three times.

The Master moved on and Hamnet rubbed his smarting hand and tried to concentrate for the remainder of the lesson. The bell rang and the boys stood in silence while the Master led the prayers then left the schoolroom, followed by the usher. As soon as he had gone, there was an instant outburst of noise. Hamnet grabbed his books and fled.

A hand seized his arm.

'Hi.'

Hamnet turned. 'Cal!'

'Where's Sturley?'

'Gone away with father to Coventry to rejoin the players. They went at daybreak.'

Cal relaxed. 'He came for me.'

'Who? Master Sturley? Last night?'

'Yep.'

'Was there a fight?' Hamnet asked eagerly. 'It looked as if there had been one. The straw was tossed everywhere.'

'Not much of one,' Cal said ruefully. 'He's bigger than me.'

'What happened?'

Cal shrugged. 'I got away.'

'I wish I'd been there,' Hamnet said enviously. 'Where did you go? I looked round the garden and in all the barns.'

'I went back to my own time.'

'Your own time?' He caught Cal's sleeve in excitement. 'Then you've brought the manuscript?'

There was a moment's silence.

'No.'

'Why not?'

Cal spoke bitterly. 'It's been stolen. It was pinched from my grip while I was bathing. I'm sorry.'

'Stolen in *your* time? But why? Of what value is one of my father's plays in your time?'

Cal glanced at him. 'It's probably worth a lot more than Sturley would get for it.'

Hamnet looked puzzled.

'Look,' Cal said. 'Your father is just about the most famous playwright in the world. Everyone's heard of him. They even teach him at school. Why, if a play of his turned up, one that no one knew about, people would pay a fortune for it.'

Hamnet let out his breath slowly. 'This is in truth?'

'Sure.'

'Do you know who's taken it?'

'I guess so.'

They had moved into the shelter of the entrance to the Guild Chapel while they had been speaking. Suddenly Cal gripped Hamnet's arm.

'Say, who's that?'

Hamnet turned to see a black-gowned figure striding past and on down the street.

'That's the Master.'

'Your teacher?'

'Yes. Why?'

Cal stared after him. 'I'm sure he's the man in black I saw at the inn. The one who handed the manuscript over to Sturley.'

'Is he?' Hamnet said thoughtfully. He watched for a moment, then slipped out of the entrance and cautiously began to follow him. Cal went after.

'His name is Barnard,' Hamnet explained under his breath. 'He's only a temporary Master and has not been at school long. He came from Oxford, Corpus Christi College. He's not liked.' He grinned. 'But then no Master is.'

'Why are we following him?' Cal asked. 'He hasn't got the manuscript.'

'Maybe not, but if you are right he must have played a part in its theft.'

Anthony Barnard walked down to the river, then turned right along the Bankcroft, which was the common land used for grazing cattle and sheep. The river stretched away to their left, past barns and farmland. Ahead of them was the church with its short wooden spire.

'Where do you think he's going?' Cal asked quietly.

'To his lodging maybe.'

'Do you know where that is?'

'No. Wait—yes, I do. Judith said he has lodgings in Mill Lane.'

As they watched, the figure disappeared inside the church. Cal and Hamnet halted.

'Why's he gone there?' Cal asked.

Hamnet shrugged. 'To pray? I know not. He is a priest.'

They reached the church and hovered outside.

'His lodgings are not far from here . . . ' Hamnet said thoughtfully. He glanced at Cal, then turned down the lane running along the side of the church. Cal followed.

The house in which Anthony Barnard had his lodging was tall and narrow. An open door led directly to a long flight of stairs. Hamnet stopped outside its entrance and looked around. The lane was deserted.

'Wait for me here,' said Hamnet.

'Hey, hold on a minute. What are you going to do?'

'Search his room.'

'What for?'

'Proof of his theft,' Hamnet said coolly. He turned towards the entrance but Cal grabbed his arm.

'Hold on. The proof won't be there. The proof is the manuscript and that's in my time, not yours.'

'Aye, but there must be something . . . ' Hamnet was frowning, 'some link with Sturley.' He looked up and his face was serious. 'There is a plot growing around my father and I like it not.'

'Okay,' Cal agreed, 'but I'll go search.'

Hamnet looked rebellious. 'It's my business not yours.'

'Yeah, but I'm in it as deep as you.'

'We'll go together.'

'No. One of us should keep watch.' He looked at Hamnet's stubborn face and felt suddenly protective towards him. 'C'mon. It's just plain common sense. Neither of us knows what we're looking for and he doesn't know me. It'd be tough on you if you were caught.'

'I'm not afraid!'

Cal grinned. 'Sure you're not.'

For a moment Hamnet glowered obstinately, then he grinned back. 'Very well. I'll hoot like an owl if I see him coming.'

'Fine,' said Cal, relieved. He stepped over the threshold, pausing a moment to accustom his eyes to the dim light. Then he mounted the steep flight of steps and gently tried the door at the top of the landing. It was not locked. Quietly he pushed it open.

The tiny room was dark, lit only by one small, grimy window. It smelt of dirty clothes and stale food. Cal wrinkled his nose and looked around. There were books everywhere, stacked from floor to ceiling, piled high up the walls, on the chairs, and strewn over the unmade bed. The one table was covered with yet more books, innumerable papers, and the mouldy remains of at least two meals.

His first thought was to leave, for he would never find anything among this mess. Besides, he was not at all sure that there *was* anything to find. Then he remembered Hamnet. If he left without making even a cursory search, Hamnet would think it poor-spirited and insist on looking for himself. Cal took a cautious step inside. It was very quiet. He hesitated for a moment then moved resolutely towards the table.

'And how may I help you?'

Cal remained frozen for a second, then spun around. A tall, dark figure stood framed in the doorway.

Anthony Barnard entered the room, a look of mild enquiry on his thin face. 'I am afraid my room is not fit for entertaining . . . ' He picked up a pile of books from a stool and looked round helplessly. 'I do try to keep order but I am inept in the art . . . And Mistress Swift does not always take the care she should . . . ' His voice trailed away. He dumped the books on the floor, picked up the stool and, with a shy, almost hesitant smile, offered it to Cal. 'Pray be seated.'

Cal blinked, took the proffered stool without thinking and sat down. He watched while Barnard removed his cloak, threw it on the bed, then leant wearily against the side of the table. He was a big, bony man with a long, gaunt face, criss-crossed with deep lines. With his hunched shoulders and long neck he looked like an evil black crow, but there was nothing in the least bit sinister about his clumsy, rather awkward movements, and his dark, close-set eyes showed nothing more alarming than a mild and courteous interest. Suddenly Barnard frowned.

'You are not one of my pupils?'

Cal shook his head.

'I thought not, although I am not yet wholly acquainted with all of them. There are so many . . . ' he sighed. 'Your name, young sir?'

'C—Cal. Calvin.'

'Well then, Master Calvin, how may I help you?'

Cal swallowed and tried to think of something to say. His initial fright had given way to acute embarrassment. Somehow he had got it all wrong. This guy was nothing like the sinister figure he had imagined.

'Perhaps you wish to be enrolled at the school?' Barnard asked helpfully. 'You seem a little old, however . . . Of what age are you?'

'Fourteen,' Cal replied automatically.

Barnard began shaking his head. 'I am afraid . . . '

'No,' Cal said hurriedly. 'No, it's not that. I—uh . . . '

Barnard was looking at him with his head on one side. 'Your speech is interesting. I have not heard its like before.'

Cal stood up. 'Yeah, well, I'd better get going. I—I guess I made a mistake . . . '

'A mistake?'

'I . . . well, I thought I'd seen you before.'

'I see!' Anthony Barnard beamed. 'And you thought to renew our acquaintance. How kind. Do, pray sit down.'

Cal sat once more, his face flushed, while Barnard continued to beam at him, the smile faltering as a worried look came into his eyes.

'Pray forgive me—my memory is very poor—I cannot quite recall the circumstance of our meeting . . . '

'No,' Cal stammered. 'We've never met. I just—just thought I'd seen you there—in London—in an inn. And . . . and you were with an actor . . . ' he trailed off miserably.

The result was surprising. Barnard straightened himself and his pale face became flushed with pink.

'Oh. I see. With an actor. Yes.' He cleared his throat, and began to speak in a slightly hectoring voice, as if delivering a lecture. 'I cannot denounce, as some of my puritan brothers do, the performing of plays.' He started to pace up and down the room, his long black robe sweeping the books and papers around him into fresh disorder.

'I cannot believe, as has been written, that plays corrupt youth and are the cause of sin, or that players have enslaved themselves to the devil and are thus condemned in the hereafter to the torments of Hell.' He stopped abruptly in front of Cal and held up his hand. 'If the good Queen herself approves them we, her loyal subjects, should surely bow our heads in submission. My consorting with players is, or should be, of no matter.'

'I didn't mean . . . gee, I don't know what you're talking about,' Cal said, completely bewildered. 'I just . . . I just saw you hand over a package to one of the actors and then I saw you here, and Hamnet said you were his teacher and . . . and I thought . . . '

Barnard's face cleared. 'Ah, so you are a friend of Hamnet!' he said delightedly. 'Why did you not say? So that was why he was standing at the top of the lane when I came past. He was making strange noises. I did not think to ask what he was doing there, but sent him home.' He pulled a chair forwards, dumped its contents on to the floor and sat down. 'And you wish to know about the manuscript? Of course, of course, there is no mystery! I told young Mistress Shakespeare that only yesterday but she seemed uncommonly distraught.'

'Mistress Shakespeare?' Cal repeated slowly.

'Mistress Judith.' He smiled, and settled his long limbs more comfortably in the chair. 'She knows of my interest in plays, an interest considered unworthy by some, but one I have held to for many years.' He leaned forward confidingly. 'I would, Master Cal, have been a player myself, but my late father . . . ' he sighed. 'Well, all that is past. Besides, I doubt I have the talent,' he added sadly. 'But whenever my duties permit, I travel to London to see the plays enacted. I myself am a poet. Oh, naught besides such

108

as Master Shakespeare and the late Master Marlowe, of course, although I strive constantly for improvement.' He jumped to his feet. 'But I am discourteous. You will take some ale?'

Cal shook his head. 'No. No, thank you.'

'Forgive me if I do. Teaching gives a thirst.' He poured out a drink from the jug on the table and returned to his chair.

'I was enchanted when Mistress Judith lent me the manuscript of Master Shakespeare's new play. I took the greatest care of it and read it on my journey to London. I attended the theatre—saw an excellent performance of *The Merchant of Venice*—and later became acquainted with Master Sturley in a nearby hostelry. He had played the part of Launcelot Gobbo, a servant to Shylock, and I complimented him on his performance. Over a jug or two of ale, we conversed on the merits of this play and that, and I told him of the one I had just read. He professed a desire to read it and kindly offered to return it to Master Shakespeare himself. As he was a player with "The Lord Chamberlain's Men" I naturally did not hesitate to trust him. I therefore arranged to meet him the following evening and gave him the manuscript.'

He stopped and looked at Cal, as if expecting a response. Cal said nothing. Anthony Barnard sighed wistfully. 'I would have liked, above all things, to have met with Master Shakespeare, but I did not wish to trouble Master Sturley for an introduction. I could have asked Hamnet or Mistress Judith to introduce me, indeed I sometimes hope that Mistress Judith might do so, but . . . ' he smiled apologetically. 'I am by nature a rather timid man, I must confess, and I must own that the thought of meeting such a dazzling talent as Master Shakespeare's rather overawes a humble schoolteacher.'

They sat for a moment in silence. At last Anthony Barnard rubbed his hand in a puzzled fashion across his face. 'I am at a loss to understand it. Mistress Judith seemed much distressed when I told her I had returned the manuscript. And now you come seeking news of it . . . ' He looked at Cal with sad, worried eyes. 'I trust I did naught amiss . . . '

Chapter Ten

'*Why* did you do it, Judith?' Hamnet exploded, swinging himself down from the branch of the apple tree.

'And then not tell us?' Susanna followed up in milder tones.

They were meeting in their accustomed place at the far end of the garden beside the big barn, and Cal had just finished telling his story.

Judith sat composedly on the bank, almost as if she had not heard. After a moment's silence she looked at Cal but she spoke to Hamnet who was now standing rigidly in front of her.

'And you believe the stranger, do you, brother?'

'Of course!'

Judith shrugged. 'Then there's nothing more to be said.'

Hamnet was red-faced with anger. 'Nothing more to be said? Indeed there is! *Why*, Judith? Why did you take it secretly when you know that father would have lent it to you for the asking? Why give it to Master Barnard? Why say naught of this during all our discussions? Oh, there's a lot more to be said!'

Judith glanced at Hamnet; a small, amused glance.

'All right,' she said in an indifferent voice. 'I did take it. I don't deny it.'

'But *why*?' cried Susanna.

Judith looked at her. 'Why? Oh, a thousand reasons.' She glanced at Hamnet. 'You wonder why I didn't ask father. You know what he would have said had I done so? "Why, child, what would you want with it? You cannot even read."'

Hamnet and Susanna exchanged looks.

111

'He would have patted me absentmindedly on the head, as if I had been a lap dog, and bid me go and play. And then he would have forgotten all about me.'

'That's not true!' Hamnet said hotly.

'Oh, it is. Look how he forgot me last night when he was introducing his family to Master Sturley.'

'He was tired then,' Hamnet said defensively.

There was a small, uncomfortable silence.

'He loves us all, Judith,' Susanna said quietly.

'Oh aye, maybe. But he loves *you* because you are the eldest, and Hamnet because he is the son and heir. I have nothing to offer and have always been naught . . .'

Hamnet frowned impatiently and opened his mouth to speak, but shut it again after a sharp look from Susanna. She went over to Judith and put her arm about her. Judith shrugged her off and turned away towards the garden. The silence was broken by Cal.

'But, I don't get it. *Why* did you give it to Barnard?'

Judith hesitated. 'He was interested to read it,' she said indifferently.

'How well do you know Master Barnard, Judith?' Susanna asked quietly.

'He was teaching me to read and write. We met after I had been on an errand to Master Sadler at the Mill. He walked with me and talked—oh, about all kinds of things,' her face softened. 'He is so learned and wise . . .'

'Why did he talk to *you* then?' Hamnet interrupted rudely. 'You're only a child!'

'So are you, *twin*!' Judith flashed back at him. 'Master Barnard did not treat me as a child. He said I had a—a natural intelligence which it was pity to waste . . .'

Hamnet gave a snort of laughter and Judith flushed angrily.

'You must not think, Cal, that Judith has been badly treated,' Hamnet explained. 'Susanna and Judith used to attend Petty School and Susanna can read and write. Our good Queen Elizabeth sets the highest standard for learning among women. Judith was just too stupid to master her letters.'

'Peace, Hamnet!' Susanna said sharply.

'Aye, hold your tongue!' Judith exclaimed angrily. 'He was the only person ever to take an interest in me! He promised to teach me Latin.'

'And did he so?' Susanna asked curiously.

'He gave me one lesson,' Judith said.

'But what of the *manuscript*?' Hamnet demanded.

'He talked a lot about father. He admires him greatly and asked what work he was engaged on . . .'

'. . . and you, like the fool you are, told him!' Hamnet broke in. 'Father is always warning us of theft and telling us how jealously the companies guard their plays!'

'But that is in London, not here,' Judith said impatiently. 'And besides, Master Barnard is not connected with any players. He is a priest and a scholar.'

Susanna stirred. 'But from what Cal has told us, Master Barnard *is* connected with the players.'

'Well, never mind all that,' Hamnet said irritably. He turned again to Judith. 'So when you told him about *Love's Labour's Won*, he asked you to steal it, did he?'

'It wasn't like that at all! He just said he greatly desired to read it. And I—I thought it was something I could do in return . . .'

'Why could he not ask father?' Susanna asked.

'The matter never arose! You don't understand!' Judith's voice rose. 'He is not an evil man—he is not in some plot with Master Sturley—he was just . . . kind to me . . .'

'So like a simpleton you gave him father's new play, and he gave it to Master Sturley and because of it we're all caught in this pretty coil,' Hamnet said disgustedly. 'You are a fool, Judith!'

'Hey, come on.' Cal had been silent for so long that they all turned to him in astonishment. 'Come on, you guys.

She's not the only one to have messed things up. I'm the one who was meant to help and all I've done is take the manuscript into my own time and then let it get stolen. You should be having a go at me, rather than her.'

There was a long silence. Hamnet sat down resignedly on the bank and began to tear up the turf with his dagger.

'Why did you not tell us, Judith?' Susanna said gently. 'You let us talk and worry and you said nothing, even after I visited Mistress Bromley. Why did you not speak?'

'I couldn't,' Judith muttered.

Susanna sighed and began to pick abstractedly at some blades of grass. Hamnet was still playing with his dagger, so it was only Cal who happened to look up and see the fleeting glance that Judith gave to her brother and sister. It was a strange, almost triumphant glance and it was gone in an instant. And then Cal understood.

It had been a short-lived triumph. A fleeting revenge. The moment when she had held the key to the mystery, which had been no mystery at all. She had no doubt sat back and enjoyed their anxiety, enjoyed seeing Hamnet's bright confidence for once clouded with the insecurity which was so much part of her own life. Cal could understand insecurity. So she had hugged the knowledge she possessed . . . until it had all got out of hand.

Perhaps she had intended to 'discover' the manuscript when Barnard returned it to her and bask in their thanks. Perhaps she would have taken the play straight to her father in the hope of winning some words of praise.

But it had all gone wrong when Cal had turned up. No wonder she had taken such a dislike to him and been so resentful of his presence. And then, he thought pityingly, what must she have felt when Barnard told her that he had given the manuscript to Sturley?

Judith caught his glance. Her face reddened and tears came to her eyes.

'It's okay,' he said quietly. 'It's okay.'

She caught her breath and her eyes widened for a moment, then she looked down quickly and began to pick at a loose thread in her skirt.

Susanna stirred. 'Well. It was ill done of you, Judith, but you know that. The manuscript is gone and cannot, it seems, be brought back. What is to be done now?'

'I will tell father,' Judith said in a small voice.

'No!' Hamnet spoke quickly. 'I'll tell him. My carelessness was to blame.'

'Hey, wait a minute,' Cal said.

The three turned towards him.

'Confessing is all very well, but that doesn't get the manuscript back,' Cal said slowly, thinking as he spoke. 'Look, I know I've made a hash of it so far, but give me another chance before you tell him.' He stopped for a moment. 'The manuscript's been stolen from me, okay? In my own time, right? And I *know*—at least I've a darn good idea—who's taken it. Just give me a chance to get it back, will you?'

He looked round at the faces staring at him: Susanna was looking doubtful, Hamnet, surprised, while Judith . . . Judith's face showed understanding.

It was to Judith he spoke, no longer thinking now, words pouring out, tumbling over one another in his effort to explain, be understood, for he was championing her cause as well as his own and he wanted her to know it.

'Where I come from you're nothing if you don't succeed. My dad never did—he's a university lecturer, but he's a failure really, he never stood up to Mum and that's why . . .' He stopped, horrified at the torrent of words that had come pouring forth, out of control. He took a deep breath and began again.

'Look, I admire your dad, I really do. He's a success story and, where I come from, that's all that matters, believe me. I don't know why I was sent here but it's my

115

chance, you see, my chance to succeed, my chance to prove I can do *something*!' He stopped again, his face flushed and sweating, his throat aching with all that was still to be said. 'I figured you were dead against his finding out,' he finished lamely.

'That was before,' Hamnet said slowly. 'Now it seems that to tell him is the only honourable thing to do.'

'Well, that's all very well,' Cal said with an effort, for his voice seemed to be sticking in his throat and the words were hard to say. Sweat was pouring down his face, into his eyes, blurring his vision. 'That's all very well, but give me just one more chance first. Just one . . . I guess . . . I guess . . .'

The words were slurring over each other, impossible to get out, impossible to understand, becoming as indistinct as the three people staring at him. The harder he tried, the more they were slipping away, growing dim and hazy as their outlines blurred into the shadow of the apple tree . . .

. . . and merged into the shoppers and tourists in Bridge Street . . .

Cal could see the small figure of Nicky running away from him, darting between people and traffic until she was lost from sight. He stared after her, too shaken to attempt pursuit, then he stood up and slowly began to walk home.

He caught John Loveday on the steps of the guest house, just as he was leaving.

'Mr Loveday—sir—I'd like a word.'

'Now, Cal? Can't it wait?' John was irritable. 'I'm already late for a meeting.'

'No, sir, it can't wait.'

He glanced at Cal's set face. 'Oh, very well. Five minutes then.' He turned sharply. 'Come into the lounge.'

'I'd like somewhere private, sir.'

John glanced back at him, amused. 'This *does* sound serious,' he said lightly. 'We'll use Mrs Walters' sitting room. She's out shopping.'

He led the way into the small, immaculately-clean but heavily over-furnished sitting room of the proprietor of the guest house. Every surface was crowded with knick-knacks and bric-à-brac. It seemed as if Mrs Walters had crammed every loved possession into this tiny area in order to save them from potentially destructive guests.

John looked round and shuddered, 'God, what awful taste.' He sat down on a well-stuffed armchair and motioned Cal to the settee. 'Now then, what's your problem?'

Cal sat down slowly. How, he wondered suddenly, should he begin? He could not accuse Loveday outright of theft, not without proof. Perhaps he should have gone about it differently, talked to Nicky maybe, followed the guy . . . Perhaps, after all, he had got it wrong . . .

'Well?' The voice was smooth, amused, lightly sarcastic.

'Where's the manuscript?' Cal asked bluntly.

'What manuscript?' John scarcely attempted to show surprise.

'You know. The manuscript of *Love's Labour's Won* which you, or your accomplice, stole from my locker when I was swimming.'

'My dear Cal . . .'

'I know you're Nicky's brother and I know she told you everything about it,' Cal went on hotly. 'You spied on us and saw me show her the manuscript and you knew it was genuine and that I'd been back into Shakespeare's time. You wanted it, didn't you, so you stole it from me. Well, I just want you to know that I'm wise to you, okay, you and Wantage, and you're not going to get away with it.' He ran out of breath and stopped. John was looking at him with curious interest.

'And just what do you propose to do?' he asked.

'Do?' Cal was unprepared for this. 'I—I'm going to try and get it back from you and if that fails I'll make sure you don't get any reward from it.'

'Very well,' said John. 'Let's not fence with each other. I am not for a moment accepting that what you say is anything more than the ill-thought out imaginings of a childish, over-stimulated brain, but, within these four walls and without witnesses, let us suppose that you are right. The manuscript is safe, my dear Cal, and I don't see that there is anything you can do about it.'

Cal was trembling with anger. 'Just you wait,' he said. 'Just wait until you try to sell it.'

John sighed. 'You really are a most tiresome boy. Of all the difficult, surly adolescents it's been my misfortune to shepherd around, you've been the worst. You think I like being a guide and teacher? You think I like trying to stretch your little minds and inculcate something of the golden literary heritage of this country?' He laughed shortly. 'Still, it's not a bad way of earning some cash. It supplements the grant, until something better turns up, of course. I repeat, Cal, given that your suppositions are correct, I just don't see what you can do about it.'

'Oh, don't you?' Cal said in a choking voice. 'I'll tell. I'll tell everything!'

John laughed. 'And what, precisely, will you tell? That I, or my accomplice, as you so quaintly term him, stole the manuscript? Oh, and who will you tell? The police? Your father?'

There was a moment's silence.

'So, you will go to the police. "And what proof have you got?" they will say, quite politely. "What proof?"' He was watching Cal narrowly as he spoke. Cal did not stir and John, satisfied, went on smoothly.

'They will then ask, "And how did *you* obtain this famous manuscript?" "Oh," you'll reply "I stole it myself." "Did you now?" they'll say, less politely. "And when was this?" "In 1596," you'll reply, that is, if you persist in the fairy-tale with which you've stuffed my sister's head. And do you think they'll believe you, Cal—do you honestly?'

118

Anger flooded through Cal. 'It's not a fairy-tale and the manuscript doesn't belong to you—or to me! It belongs to Shakespeare and—and—to the world. You only want it for the money you can make . . . !'

'No!' John spoke sharply. 'Not the money, although I admit that is an attraction. But I told you before, Cal, the real attraction is in possession . . . in owning such a thing even for a short time . . .'

His breathing was shallow and fast and there was an intent look on his face. With difficulty he controlled himself and looked dispassionately at Cal.

'We never had this conversation, Cal, and I know nothing at all about what you are saying.' He stood up. 'I must warn you, however, that if you make any more unsubstantiated allegations of theft it would be seriously to your disadvantage. You are, after all, in a foreign country.' He walked over to the door. 'Come, I've given you enough of my time already.'

Cal stood reluctantly, angry and mortified. He wanted to hit out, to hurt . . . but he did nothing except compose his face into a mask of sullen indifference. John looked at him curiously.

'Just off the record, Cal, how *did* you obtain that manuscript? You might as well tell me, you know.'

'I went back into the past,' Cal said with rigid dignity.

John's eyes narrowed. 'Well—if, by some unaccountable chance you *are* telling me the truth, I must say I envy you,' he said. 'Though why *you* should have had such an experience is past my comprehension.'

He held the door open and Cal walked stiffly past him and out into the hall.

Chapter Eleven

The pub opposite the Royal Shakespeare Theatre was named The Black Swan, although it was generally known as The Dirty Duck. It was a favourite haunt of actors and anyone who wanted to see and be seen. Early that evening, at the height of the tourist season, it was very full. The hot weather meant that the majority of people were outside, squashed on to the small raised terrace in front of the pub.

Seated on the wall, his back to the street, Richard Wantage looked up as John stood at the top of the steps.

'Over here!'

John pushed his way through the crowd. 'Can't we go somewhere more private?'

Richard shrugged. 'It's as good as anywhere and there's more privacy in a crowd. Here.' He pushed a pint along the wall. 'Sit down, man, and stop looking so worried.'

John sat and absentmindedly took a drink.

'Why the urgent summons?'

John was silent for a moment. 'It's that meddling kid,' he said at last.

'The one I half drowned?'

'Yes.'

'Pity I didn't finish the job then,' Richard said with a grin.

'It's no laughing matter,' John said tensely.

'Who's laughing?'

'Look, he knows everything and what he doesn't know he's guessed.'

Richard shrugged. 'So what can he do? If he tries telling anyone, who'd believe him?'

'That's what I told him,' John said grimly. 'Tried to frighten the little devil, but I'm not sure he believed me. He's brighter than I gave him credit for.'

120

'So what do you propose?' Richard glanced at him and raised an eyebrow. 'My dear man, you surely aren't suggesting . . .?'

John was startled. 'No, of course not.'

'That would, of course, be the simplest solution, but in this day and age . . .? I don't somehow think we'd stand a chance of getting away with it.' Richard laughed. 'It was easier in Shakespeare's time, of course—a quick knife between the ribs then slip the evidence into the Avon and no one any the wiser.'

John shuddered. 'I abhor violence of any kind,' he said stiffly.

'Do you?' Richard laughed again. 'I can't say I do. Not if the stakes are high enough.'

John leaned forwards. 'Look—will you take it? He goes home the day after tomorrow and with a bit of luck he'll forget all about it. Even if he doesn't, he won't be able to do us any harm. Until then, there's no telling what the little fool might try. Or my sister, for that matter. She seems to be in league with him,' John added bitterly. 'It'll be safer with you.'

Richard hesitated for a moment. 'Aren't you making a mountain out of the proverbial molehill?'

There was a moment's silence.

'I don't know. Possibly.'

'Well, I'm happy to take it—if you're sure you trust me.' He glanced at John and grinned. 'I might double-cross you, you know.'

'Of course I trust you,' John said impatiently. 'We're in this together, aren't we?' He sipped at his drink thoughtfully. 'But perhaps you're right and I'm worrying over nothing. If you feel there's no danger . . .'

'Oh, there's danger,' Richard said shortly. 'And I for one won't feel safe until our story is accepted, the manuscript authenticated and sold at auction to the highest bidder.'

John sighed. 'I suppose it must go for auction?'

Richard put down his glass. 'My dear man . . .'

'It's just . . . to see it go out of the country . . . '

'There's no certainty it will. Perhaps the money will be forthcoming to keep it here. Perhaps some public benefactor will buy it for the nation. It's happened before. Look at the Mappa Mundi.' He drained his glass. 'Anyway I don't really care as long as I make a fortune out of it.' He glanced at John. 'And I don't see why *you* should worry as long as you get your fair share,' he added.

'I don't care for the money.'

'Don't you?'

John flushed and was silent.

'Maybe you *are* as altruistic as you make out. I don't know. But you care for the glory of having discovered it, don't you? You can't deny that.'

'No.'

'Cold feet?'

'Of course not!'

Richard put down his glass. 'I've got to go. The performance starts soon and Bottom's make-up takes forever.' He stood up. 'Well, are you going to give it to me?'

John looked up at him. 'What will you do with it?'

'Keep it safe, of course. Do you think I'd leave it in my dressing room?'

John took the package from his briefcase and handed it over.

'And we'll go to London . . .?'

'On Sunday as we agreed, after you've seen the little darlings off on their plane.' Richard pressed his hand lightly on John's shoulder. 'Come on, man, cheer up. It's not every day you hand over a priceless document.'

Then he was gone, pushing his way through the crowded terrace, down the steps and along the pavement.

A shadow detached itself from the foot of the wall and scurried away in the opposite direction. It had been worth the risk. Now Cal knew where the manuscript was. But how on earth was he to recover it?

Greg peered anxiously at his reflection in the mirror as he combed back his sandy hair with unusual care.

'Think I'll make it tonight, you guys?'

'Make what?' muttered Gene, speaking from inside the depths of a crisply clean shirt.

Greg looked at the results of his labours and pulled a face. His hair would never be anything but thin and stringy. He turned away from the mirror.

'*It.* With Lou.'

Franklin, who was sprawled across his bed reading a comic, looked up. 'With Lou? Tonight? You got to be joking. We're going to the theatre, you dumbhead, not to a high school hop!'

'Yeah, well, but it's Shakespeare, isn't it? And Lou likes Shakespeare.'

'So you think some of that liking's going to rub off on you, do you?'

Greg was silent and returned to staring at his worried face in the mirror.

Gene nudged Franklin with his foot. 'C'mon, Fatso, you're going to make us late.'

Franklin sighed. 'Okay, okay. And won't "The Stiff" have something to say about that!'

'Not for much longer,' Gene said exultantly. 'Soon be home. Boy, will I be glad to get on that plane. Yee-haa!' He pushed his arm through the sleeve in his shirt and punched the air with his fist. 'Dad said he'd get tickets to the baseball match next weekend. You going, Cal?'

Cal was lying flat on his bed, arms behind his head, staring up at the ceiling.

'What's that?'

'Baseball match. Tickets are said to be like gold dust.'

There was a pause. 'Don't reckon.'

It had been a frustrating day. Cal had intended to go to the Royal Shakespeare Theatre and hang around the stage door in the hope that he would see Richard Wantage, but John had foiled that plan by announcing at breakfast that he had arranged a special visit to Warwick Castle. There had been no chance to sneak off before the coach had arrived and John had virtually frog-marched him on to it before he could think of escape. His only chance now lay at the theatre.

Something landed on his chest.

'Letter for you,' Lou called out from the door. Cal opened it absentmindedly. His mother wrote just as she spoke.

'. . . I guess things are pretty difficult right now. Some of his high and mighty university friends have cut me dead though the Lord knows he's the guilty party. Cy says I mustn't let it get to me, after all *I* wasn't the one who walked out. Still, I'm glad *you're* having fun at any rate, and I can't wait to see you and hear all about it, so don't go forgetting anything. Cy's managed to get tickets for that big match the weekend after you get home and I thought the three of us could go and have a fun time together and maybe take in a movie after. Cy's been a *good* friend to me, Cal, and I'm sure you'll both hit it off. Don't forget, honey, that the flags'll be flying just as soon as that plane lands. Your ever loving Mom.'

Cal crumpled the airmail sheets into a ball and hurled it across the room. It hit the wall and fell silently to the floor. Everyone stopped what they were doing and stared. Cal got wearily to his feet, hunched his shoulders and glowered at his room-mates.

'Know what you guys look like?' he asked.

'Yeah,' said Gene complacently. 'Swell.'

'A load of creeps. Hell if I'm gonna get changed!'

124

He walked out of the room and slammed the door behind him.

'I trust you all know how to behave at a theatre, but, if not, I will just go over the salient points. You are not to talk during the performance, or whisper or distract those around you in any way. I don't want to see you fidgeting or eating—so if you would care to remove whatever it is you have been chewing for the last ten minutes, Greg, I would be obliged.'

'My gum ain't goin' to annoy anyone,' Greg protested.

'That is immaterial.'

'We do have theatres in the States, you know,' said Lou resentfully.

'Oh, save your breath, Lou, he thinks we're some kind of morons. Nothing we say's going to change his mind.'

'If that is all understood, we'll go in,' said John, ignoring this. 'Cal, you have distinguished yourself this evening by being the most slovenly dressed person in this theatre. I hope you are satisfied?'

Cal did not answer.

'I am half inclined to send you home to change.'

Cal shrugged. There was a moment's silence then John sighed and turned to the rest of the group.

'You should understand the text, being high school students, but if not, there is a résumé of the plot given in the programme. Come this way.'

The group were standing in the foyer, uncomfortably aware of the amused glances being thrown at them. Thankfully they followed John through the entrance to the stalls.

Their seats were good ones, near enough to see the performance undisturbed, far enough away to be able to see the whole sweep of the stage without craning their necks. Cal was on the end of one row, John immediately behind him.

125

The stage had no curtains and was bare of props. Cal heard John mutter something but paid no attention. His head felt tight and the talking and laughter around him, the expectant buzz as people found their seats and settled themselves for the performance, jarred his nerves. He was too hot. Irritably, he pulled off his sweat-shirt and stretched his legs out into the aisle. The house lights dimmed and the performance began.

Cal was only hazily aware of the early scenes. He was conscious of feeling wound-up, like a spring that has been coiled too tightly. All his senses were alert. The sudden noise of an electronic watch high up in the circle sent his head jerking round with an abruptness that cricked his neck. A short while later, Franklin's muttered comment and Carole's quiet reply had him saying 'Shush!' with a sharpness that would have done credit to John Loveday.

Perhaps he should sneak out and try to find the dressing rooms. He turned his head and caught a glimpse of John, seated, like a gaoler, directly behind him. He could almost feel the eyes boring into the back of his head, and sense the tension in the man, tension as great as his own. Any attempt on his part to leave would be quickly thwarted. Besides, he remembered hearing Richard say that he would not keep the manuscript in his dressing room. Cal abandoned the idea.

Where would he keep it then? In his house? How could Cal find out where he lived? If he could manage to slip away after the performance and hang around the theatre until the actor left, he could follow him home, Cal reasoned. Apart from packing, the next day was free until the early evening flight, so he might just get an opportunity to take the manuscript if only he could keep a close watch. If not, Nicky might help—if only he knew where to find her. He clenched his teeth in frustration and stared at the stage.

The play moved from the Athenian court to the house of Quince for the first of the comedy scenes. The actors entered. Cal sat bolt upright in nervous anticipation as his eyes followed Richard Wantage—in the guise of Bottom the Weaver—on to the stage.

The scene progressed. Quince handed round pages of script while Bottom strutted boastfully about the stage. The audience warmed to the scene, laughing as Bottom snatched the sheets of paper intended for the other actors in his desire to play the best part.

'Let me play the lion too: I will roar, that I will do any man's heart good to hear me; I will roar, that I will make the duke say, "Let him roar again, let him roar again".'

And then Cal knew.

He felt the tension rising in his body until it seemed intolerable to remain seated in his chair. There was a surging in his ears and a voice which he did not recognize as his own, shouting:

'Stop! Stop the performance!'

There was a rustling around him of which he was hardly aware as he jumped to his feet and ran down the aisle towards the stage. All Cal knew was that this was the time, this was when he would succeed, this was his own moment of glory . . . Without conscious thought he leapt on to the stage and raced towards the papers held in Richard's hands.

He took the actor in a flying tackle, knocking him to the floor. The papers fell around him. Cal knelt and feverishly began to collect them up. There was a rising crescendo of sound and hands grasped at his back. He grabbed the last paper, shook off the restraining hands and fled off the stage into the dim light of the wings. His breath was coming in short bursts.

'Here! Here you!'

A burly figure moved in front of him, arms outstretched. Cal thrust the papers inside his shirt and took a step backwards.

Pain exploded in his head and he could feel himself falling . . .

Someone caught his arm in a steadying grip.

'Hold hard, lad, don't knock yourself out.'

Cal rubbed the back of his head and tried to get his eyes into focus.

'I know you're excited, we all are, but you're not on yet.'

Cal whipped round to find himself staring into the mild face of Thomas Vincent.

'Wh . . . what?'

'Get your costume in a muck sweat and there'll be the devil to pay. Master Burbage is most particular, especially when we're appearing at Court. Now sit you down nice and quiet and I'll call you when your cue comes. Where's the other lads?'

'I . . . I don't . . .' Cal stuttered.

'No doubt up to some mischief or other. Never mind, they'll turn up when they're needed.' He pushed Cal further into the room and sat him firmly on a wooden chest. 'You sit still for a bit. You look white as a sheet. No need to feel nervous. Our good Queen's very fond of a play.'

Cal took a deep breath and looked around. He was in a room similar to the tiring room at The Theatre in respect of the mess of costumes and props strewn everywhere, but this was different, altogether larger and grander than the tiring room Cal remembered. It was panelled in wood, and paintings hung around the walls. There were only one or two other people in the room. Cal recognized the familiar, worried figure of Peter who was on his knees putting the final touches to Titania's long white dress and train.

He put his hand to his chest and there, inside his costume, he could feel the comforting thickness of paper next to his skin. The manuscript. He had it safe. The relief was overwhelming and he closed his eyes for a second. When he opened them it was to find Sturley standing before him, a grim expression on his face.

'Come, we're on!'

Hubert, resplendent in Cobweb's pink and grey satin costume, grabbed Cal by the arm and hurried him to the door. They were joined by Ned and John, dressed as the other two fairies, and a moment later they were all walking sedately on stage behind Titania.

They entered into a blaze of light and Cal was momentarily blinded.

'*Ill met by moonlight, proud Titania.*'

The scene had begun. Later on Cal was to have little recollection of playing the part of Moth in front of Queen Elizabeth I. At the time he was conscious only of trying not to call attention to himself while on stage and of keeping out of Sturley's way when off stage. He supposed that his reading of the play must have stood him in good stead for he made no obvious mistakes, speaking Moth's few words at the appropriate moments. He was sure that he could not have made a very convincing fairy but no one appeared to notice.

The hall in which they played was enormous, stretching away into darkness. It was full of people, although Cal could glimpse nothing more than dim shapes, some seated, some standing, for the stage was surrounded by the brilliant blaze of hundreds of candles. On stage, Cal was only aware of Sturley, who watched him with hard eyes as he waited, patiently, for the play to end.

The end came at last. Candles were lit in the body of the hall and Cal stood with the other players and bowed before the applauding audience. He could see the courtiers now and the ladies of the Court, and there, on a raised dais, was the Queen herself, a fantastic jewel-encrusted figure, whose dress, with its wide hooped skirt, glinted and winked in the lights from the chandeliers. Her small head was framed inside a very stiff, white ruff.

First William Shakespeare knelt before her and kissed her hand, then Philip Sturley was called. The Queen spoke to them both before rising from her seat. Everyone in the hall rose with her and bowed and curtsied as she stepped from the dais and left by a side door. Her ladies followed.

Those remaining in the hall relaxed and a babble of voices arose. The players began to make their way to the tiring room and Sturley began to stride purposefully towards Cal.

'Good, Philip, very good. I liked your playing of the part very well.'

It was Shakespeare, throwing a companionable arm around Sturley's shoulder. Cal looked from one to the other, hesitated, then took out the wedge of papers from his doublet.

'Sir!'

Shakespeare looked round. 'Yes?' He smiled, relaxed and at ease. 'A not altogether convincing Moth, Cal, but you will improve.'

'Sir, this is yours.'

Shakespeare looked questioningly at Cal as he took the proffered sheets. Sturley, after a sudden, startled glance, disappeared quietly into the tiring room.

Cal watched with pounding heart as Shakespeare opened the pages and read swiftly. Then he looked up, puzzled.

'But what is this?'

'It's your new play, sir. *Love's Labour's Won.*'

Shakespeare was shaking his head. 'No, Cal. It is a stage property.'

Cal stared at him, shaken.

'Thomas provided it for the rehearsal scene,' Shakespeare said. 'It is worthless.' He looked suddenly at Cal. 'But what do you mean about my play? I left the manuscript with Hamnet.'

Cal wanted to answer but the weight of failure seemed to be pressing down on him, preventing him from speaking. Besides, he could no longer see Shakespeare clearly through the light of thousands of blazing candles that were streaming towards him.

The ground lurched under him, the flames merged into one glowing ball, then the walls and ceiling dissolved in a blaze of light and Cal was falling, falling . . .

Chapter Twelve

He came round to find himself seated in the foyer of the Royal Shakespeare Theatre with Carole crouched beside him.

'Say, you okay?'

'What?'

'You had some kind of fit or something. You sure caused a sensation back there.'

'What happened?'

'Don't you remember?' Carole settled herself more comfortably. 'You went rushing on to the stage shouting like you'd gone crazy, then you knocked yourself out against some scenery. They had to carry you here—you've been unconscious for ages.'

'Who did . . .?' Cal asked, coming slowly into the present.

'Security guys, I reckon. They were real mad at first but when "The Stiff" told them you were sick they calmed down. They wanted to get an ambulance, but he said you'd be all right.'

'Where's he gone?'

'Who?'

'Loveday.'

'I don't know. He went some time ago. Said he'd be back. Do you want me to find him?'

Cal frowned. 'Is the play still going on?'

'Yeah. The stage manager or something came out and apologized and it just carried on like nothing had happened. I think you made poor Loveday's glamorous actor-friend sick too, because the stage manager guy apologized for him and said the understudy would be taking over. We all wanted to go then but "The Stiff" hissed at us to stay

132

where we were. He was mad as fire. I came out after it restarted and Mr Loveday yelled at me to stay with you and not let you out of my sight. Said he'd be back soon. Sure you're okay?'

'I'm fine,' Cal said absentmindedly. He sat up. Beside him, on the seat, were some crumpled sheets of paper.

'What's that?'

Carole shrugged. 'I don't know. I guess you were holding on to them when you passed out.'

Cal picked up the top page. The paper was thick and covered with writing. He looked at it more closely. There were no words, just meaningless scribbles.

'All right, Carole, you can join the others.' John had entered quietly through the main door.

'I'm quite happy to stay, Mr Loveday.'

'Will you do what you're told, just for once?' he snapped, an edge to his voice.

'Okay, okay.' She patted Cal's shoulder in a motherly fashion and disappeared inside. John sat down heavily, dislodging the papers. They fluttered harmlessly to the floor.

'Well, Cal.'

Cal hunched up his shoulders.

'Did you really think Richard would risk using the real manuscript as a stage prop?' John asked contemptuously.

Cal shrugged.

'I would have credited you with more sense.'

Cal said nothing and they sat in silence for a moment.

'So you've won,' Cal said at last.

John did not reply for a moment.

'Oh no,' he said slowly. 'I haven't won at all.'

Cal looked at him. John's shoulders were slumped, and his lips set in a bitter line.

'What do you mean?'

John was silent.

'Say, what's happened?' Cal demanded.

John sighed. 'You might as well know.' He spoke slowly, deliberately, as if each word was an effort. 'Richard left the theatre during the interval. I was just too late. He drove off as I ran down the steps. He knew I was there for he waved and wound down the window, then shouted across at me.'

Cal did not speak.

'He shouted: *"Trust none; For oaths are straws, men's faiths are wafer-cakes, And hold-fast is the only dog, my duck."* A very apt quotation in the circumstances,' John said bitterly.

There was another pause.

'By the time I'd crossed the car park, he had gone.'

'So, what are you saying?' Cal asked, slowly.

'That I've been hoodwinked, double-crossed, what you will.'

'You mean—he's gone off with the manuscript?'

'I mean just that.'

'But—where's he gone?'

John shrugged. 'God knows. He probably organized something yesterday while I was shepherding you around Warwick Castle.'

'Can't you stop him? Do something?'

John glanced at him. 'Like what?'

'Tell the police.'

'Oh yes? Remember what I said to you? No, I've been nicely caught out. Hoist, as they say, with my own petard.'

'Well, you can't expect me to feel sorry for you!' Cal said angrily.

'Oh, I don't, believe me.'

There was silence for a moment.

'What'll he do with it?'

'I don't know. Probably sell it privately. No doubt it will go to some multi-billionaire's private collection, to be gloated over in secret and never seen again.'

'What's the point of that?'

'Possession. Owning something no one else has,' John said wearily.

134

'That's what *you* wanted!'

'No. I wanted the world to have it. But unlike you, Cal, I wanted to go down in the history books as having been the one who discovered it. I wanted fame and perhaps a tidy sum of money as well.' He hesitated a moment. 'My mistake,' he finished curtly.

A burst of applause from inside the theatre brought John to his feet.

'Come,' he said bitterly. 'I still have my job to do.'

'Hey, Cal! Cal, it's me, Nicky!'

Her voice roused him from his semi-stupor. He was lying in an easy chair in the garden of the guest house, half-dozing in the afternoon sun.

'Okay, okay, what's all the fuss?' he asked sleepily.

'I *had* to see you before you go.'

The urgency in her voice woke him fully and he looked around. They were alone in the garden, the others still wrestling with their packing or taking a final walk around Stratford.

'Why d'you want to see me?' he asked ungraciously.

'I wanted to say I was sorry.'

Cal got to his feet. 'C'mon. Let's get out of here.'

It was hotter than ever outside, the heat rising from the pavement. Cal stood in the brilliant sunshine and blinked. Rows of neat houses stretched away from him and he shaded his eyes against the hard, white glare. He began to walk slowly and Nicky pranced agitatedly at his side.

'Oh, Cal, I had to see you.'

'Well, you're seeing me now,' he said grumpily. He did not want to think about the manuscript, or Nicky, or John Loveday, or the horrendous mess he had made of everything. He had spent the whole of the night and the entire morning trying to blot it from his thoughts.

'You were right about John and I messed everything up.' Nicky's usually smiling face was solemn.

'We both screwed it up,' he said abruptly.

'I searched John's room last night when you were all at the theatre,' Nicky said . . .

'And you didn't find anything.'

'Not the manuscript—but I did find something though. There was a half-finished letter on his computer. It was to Sotheby's the auctioneers. I only glanced at it quickly because it was late and I was afraid he'd come back, but it mentioned *Love's Labour's Won.*'

Cal laughed shortly. 'Much good that'll do him.'

'But don't you *see*,' Nicky said earnestly. 'I knew then that it was all my fault. I should never have told him.'

'*I* should never have told *you*,' Cal said cruelly.

Nicky was silent for a moment. 'Can't I do something to put it right?' she asked in a small voice.

Cal stopped walking and turned to her. 'You're too late. Wantage took it. He's double-crossed your precious brother and gone off with it and now it's all over. There's nothing any of us can do.'

Her eyes grew big and round.

'Is that true?'

'Yeah.'

Nicky gulped. 'Are you very angry with me?' she asked.

'What's the use?' Cal said wearily. 'I'm more angry with myself. Look, I don't want to talk about it, okay?'

He walked on, quickening his pace and Nicky hurried to keep up.

'Do you think you'll go back into the past?'

'I doubt it. My part's over—whatever it was. I don't want to go back, anyway. I don't want to face them all.'

'But you could *explain*,' Nicky said earnestly. 'You could tell them that it wasn't your fault at all, but mine. If only I'd never told John . . .'

'If only . . .' Cal jeered. 'Never mind. It's no big thing anyway.'

'You don't mean that.'

Cal shrugged then smiled ruefully. 'No.'

Nicky opened her mouth to speak and shut it again. Suddenly she dived into the plastic bag she was carrying and brought out a small parcel.

'Here,' she said, thrusting it at Cal. 'It's nothing really, but I thought you might like it. I wrote my address inside in case you feel like writing, although you don't have to and I don't suppose you will.' She pushed it into Cal's hand. 'I'll miss you,' she said suddenly and ran off before Cal could speak.

He watched her go, surprised and a bit touched. Perhaps he had been a bit hard on her, a bit unfair.

He looked down at the parcel but did not open it immediately. He wandered down to the river, bought an ice-cream, and crossed the bridge, eating it thoughtfully.

A family were feeding some ducks and Cal stopped to watch. He stretched himself out on the bank and finished his ice-cream slowly, scrunching the last piece of wafer. The family moved off and Cal glanced down at the present which lay beside him on the grass. He picked it up and slowly removed the wrapping paper. It was a book about Shakespeare. Nice of Nicky, Cal thought, as he flicked idly through the pages. He glanced at the inscription on the flyleaf written in big round handwriting.

'*To Cal. With love from Nicky. 9th August 1993.*' Her address was underneath.

Maybe he would write to her. She wasn't a bad kid.

He skimmed over the next few pages then began to read: '*The story of William Shakespeare's life is a tale of two towns. Stratford bred him; London gave him, literally and figuratively, a stage for his fortune. In an unpretentious market town he was born and reared in a house which has miraculously survived erosions by time and tourism. Before achieving his majority he took for his bride a local girl past the bloom of youth; she bore him three children, one of whom, the only son, died young.*'

Cal stared at the page. He re-read the last few words slowly.

137

'. . . one of whom, the only son, died young.'

Hamnet? Hamnet died young? He read swiftly to the end of the page but there was nothing more about him. He turned to the back of the book and was surprised to find his hands shaking. There were only four references to Hamnet in the index. He followed them up and, in the third one, he read: '*It is reasonable to suppose that Shakespeare was there on 11 August 1596, when the parish register records the burial of his son Hamnet, aged eleven and a half. His death doomed the male line of the Shakespeares to extinction.*'

Cal looked up blindly. Hamnet? Dying? That eager boy, so alive, so full of the joy of living, dying at the age of eleven?

He curled his fingers into the grass of the bank. The heat of the summer afternoon wrapped around him and the voices of the people strolling along the path seemed distant and remote. Even the noise of the river traffic was temporarily hushed. Cal sat silent, stunned.

He *had* to get back. He had to get back to warn him, to do something . . .

A part of his brain told him that it was absurd, that they were all dead—Hamnet, Judith, Susanna, Shakespeare himself—but somehow that was not important. There seemed to be all the difference in the world between dying as an adult after a full life, and dying, as Cal had known him, a bright, shining eleven year old.

He closed his eyes and counted to ten, holding his breath, trying to re-create the dizzy feeling he had when returning to the past.

He opened his eyes and stared at the buildings on the opposite bank. They *were* growing fainter, they *must* disappear . . . he gritted his teeth and clenched his fists.

It would not work. His eyes were prickling, his heart hammering in his chest. He got to his feet and walked quickly along the bank until he reached the weir then, hot and tired, he sat down again and stared across the river.

Water tumbled down the incline and the light from the sun speckled the white froth of the waves with gold. But Cal scarcely noticed. Beads of sweat ran down his face and he felt the muscles of his body grow taut as he again tried to will himself back into the past. It was no good.

Then he saw a small figure on the far bank some little way upstream. A figure at the water's edge, peering with rapt attention into the depths of the river.

I made it, he thought, exultantly. I can do it. He tried to stand, but his limbs would not move. He looked down. His long legs in their torn jeans and dirty trainers were stretched before him on the grass. It was a second or two before realization came. He was not in the past at all.

He looked over to the far bank and it *was* Hamnet, now leaning dangerously over the water's edge. Cal could see him quite clearly. The boy's foot slipped and he grabbed hold of a branch of a tree that jutted out into the river.

'Hamnet!'

The warning voice was Cal's, although he was not aware of speaking aloud.

Hamnet looked up and shaded his hand against the sun. He waved and smiled.

'The pike!' he called excitedly, his voice echoing inside Cal's head.

Cal forced himself to stand and, once on his feet, his legs began to work normally. He ran to the bridge, keeping both eyes on Hamnet, who beckoned him on. He raced across it and began pounding up the opposite bank. Hamnet had returned to his investigation.

'Take care!'

'It's the pike!' Hamnet called again, his eyes bright with excitement.

He leaned further, holding on to the branch to steady himself.

Cal ran towards him, eyes half-blinded by sweat. He was shouting something, but no words came out.

139

There was a sudden flurry of leaves and the branch which Hamnet was holding groaned then snapped off abruptly in a small explosion of sound. Hamnet lost his footing and was thrown into the river. Cal flung himself on the bank and made a grab for the hand that reached out to his. For a second he thought he had it and he tensed, ready for the contact, ready to take tight hold of the boy and drag him to safety.

There was no contact. With a sense of shock, Cal saw his own hand pass straight through that of the boy as if there had been nothing there. His fingers closed uselessly around the empty air.

The current swiftly took Hamnet out into mid-stream. Cal caught the broken branch and flung it towards him. But the river was treacherous and the branch fell short and was swept away. The boy was being swept away too, despite his attempts to swim, for the current was proving too strong.

Shading his eyes from the sun which reflected blindingly on the water, Cal saw the small head disappear, then re-appear further down river. He jumped to his feet and raced along the bank, straining to keep the bobbing head in sight. It disappeared from view. Cal stopped and stared at the spot where he had last seen it. Nothing.

Then, much further down stream, a hand was raised, as though in salute.

And was gone . . .

Cal's eyes feverishly swept the water, but there was no further sign of the boy. The river flowed onwards, smooth and untroubled.

Cal sat on the bank and put his head in his hands. Water tumbled over the edge of the weir, foaming white and gold in the brilliant afternoon sun. Cal did not see it. A canoeist shot over the side and skilfully paddled to the calmer waters below. Cal did not notice him.

140

His cheeks were wet and there was the taste of hot salt tears on his lips. He lifted his head and sat staring across the river for a long, long time, then he stiffly climbed to his feet and began to trudge back towards the town.

Chapter Thirteen

It was getting late and Cal knew that he should be returning to the guest house, but he remained sitting on one of the benches in Henley Street watching the house which was famous as Shakespeare's birthplace.

Its upper windows were open to catch the least draught of air and there were crowds of tourists milling around the street and queuing patiently in the garden beyond the railings. People posed for photographs and video cameras in front of the building, others sat on the low wall, exhausted with sight-seeing, wearily fanning themselves with their guide-books. Groups of tourists clustered round their respective guides and there was the constant buzz of chatter in a myriad different languages. But despite all the bustle and noise which surrounded it, the house looked dead to Cal, shut in on itself.

He did not know quite what he expected, but there was nothing here, no ghosts, no prickles on his skin, no sound of Hamnet, no sight of him, nothing. He might as well go home before the coach arrived and they sent out a search party. His head throbbed and the sultry afternoon felt airless and oppressive.

In a minute, he thought, he would go in a minute.

A cool voice was speaking, the words falling softly, soothing away some of the pain.

'I will not say, do not grieve, but remember that there is nothing you could have done to save him.'

He looked up to find Susanna, a grave figure in black, standing before him.

It had been a gentle return. The tourists had gone, the paved street had reverted to a dusty, well-worn path of beaten-down earth between the overhanging houses and Cal was sitting on the edge of a water trough. Only the warmth of the late afternoon was the same.

'But I should have been able to,' Cal said simply. 'Why couldn't I return to the past when I was needed?'

Susanna shook her head. 'I don't know. I know nothing about such things.'

She took his hand and led him into the house and through it to the garden.

'I tried to warn him but I couldn't get back—not properly. I failed him now and I failed him over the manuscript,' Cal said bitterly. 'I had it and I let them take it from me.'

Susanna stopped him. 'Do not rail against yourself. The manuscript is of no matter. Father knows everything.'

'He does?'

'Yes. Hamnet and Judith told him. He was grieved that we deceived him, but not angry. He wants to thank you.' She looked at him with dark expressive eyes, her father's eyes. 'You've been a good friend to us and I shall miss you.'

Cal stared at her. 'Aren't I going to see you again?'

Susanna shook her head. 'I fear not.'

'But it's not finished!'

'It is for us. My brother's death has brought such grief to us all . . . ' Her voice broke for a moment and she stopped speaking and stared across the garden. 'Come, I see father waiting.'

They crossed to the courtyard where Shakespeare was standing expectantly, watching their approach. He was sombrely dressed in black and Cal thought he looked much older. His dark eyes were shadowed and there were deep lines etched in his face.

Susanna turned to Cal and there were tears in her eyes. 'Mistress Bromley warned us of sorrow and pain. She said that we would know the bitterness of parting. It seemed to mean nothing at the time. Perhaps we should not venture to know too much of the future or we will be unable to live our lives in peace in the present.' She stopped. 'It's always hard to say goodbye. I never realized it until lately.'

She touched his hand then went swiftly into the house. Cal watched her go.

'Sit here beside me.'

Shakespeare had moved to a bench set well back in the shelter of a rose-covered arbour.

'You wanted to see me, sir?' Cal asked tentatively.

'Yes. I have to thank you.'

Cal sat down, embarrassed. 'I didn't do anything. I was brought back here to get the manuscript but I loused everything up.'

'Who knows why you came?' Shakespeare said gently. 'Perhaps it was just to befriend my son . . . '

'I—I'm truly sorry, sir—' Cal began awkwardly.

Shakespeare stopped him with a gesture. 'Hamnet and Judith told me everything. I was grieved they had not spoken earlier, but I have also been to blame . . . ' He was silent for a moment. 'So much effort to read a play of mine. Poor Master Barnard. I should feel flattered.' He sighed. 'And my poor Judith.'

'And Philip Sturley?' Cal asked eagerly. 'What about him?'

'A rogue, Cal, the world is full of them. Greed is universal. It spans both space and time.'

'But what happened to him?'

Shakespeare shrugged. 'Why, nothing. He will not act in our company—or any other reputable company—again. I last saw him drinking himself into a wine-sodden stupor. Perhaps he will sober up when his money runs out. A pity,' he said thoughtfully. 'He could have been a good player. A sad waste of a man.' He glanced at Cal. 'He used you badly I was told.'

144

Cal flushed. 'Gee, it was nothing . . . '

'I was greatly angered when I heard. I would have pursued him with the law, but . . . there was no proof and the only witness, yourself, had vanished into thin air. And what profit is revenge? A man that studies revenge keeps his own wounds green.'

He looked at Cal, a deep, penetrating look, as if seeing him clearly for the first time. 'It is stranger still what they told me about you.'

Cal was silent.

'I doubted not their tale. The world is full of marvels. Another time, another place, Cal, and I would have wearied you with questions.' He stopped for a moment and closed his eyes wearily. 'But not now.'

Cal leaned forward. 'Sir—I *know* who has the manuscript. It could be hard getting it back, but I'd try if you want me to.'

Shakespeare opened his eyes and looked straight at Cal.

'No, Cal,' he said decidedly.

'Why not? The guy that's taken it—his name's Wantage and he's an actor too—he only wants it because he knows he can sell it and make a fortune . . . '

'Let it go.'

'But it's not fair! He shouldn't be allowed to get away with it!'

'I am sorry, but the play is now of no concern to me.'

Cal sat back, disappointed. Shakespeare watched him thoughtfully.

'This might prove hard for you to understand, Cal,' he began slowly, 'especially after everything you tried to do, but I would, at this moment, give everything I have written and everything that—if it please God—I shall write in years to come, if I could have my son alive again.'

Cal flushed. 'Yeah—sure. I—I guess I didn't think . . . '

'Cal, you knew Hamnet. You were his friend. What is a play beside the reality of him?'

There was a pause, and Cal looked down at the flagged stones of the courtyard.

Shakespeare went on earnestly. 'A play is words written in ink on parchment paper. My son was a living, breathing part of me. He was my future, my heir, my joy. If you weigh one loss against the other, the loss of the manuscript is as nothing compared with the loss of my son.' He stopped suddenly. 'I am sorry. Forgive me.'

They sat together silently. Then Shakespeare stirred.

'Time is short and I fear you must soon leave us. Thank you again.'

'I don't deserve to be thanked,' Cal said unhappily. 'I failed.'

Shakespeare looked at his bowed head. 'Success is not the only criterion, or even the most important, by which we judge events and actions. Remember that. You did not fail, even in the part of Moth.'

Cal looked up and saw warm understanding and the hint of a smile in Shakespeare's dark eyes. He blushed bright red.

'I—I'm sorry I let you down . . . '

'You did not. But neither will you, I fear, make a player. At least, not in my company.'

'No,' Cal paused, uncertain. 'Can . . . can I ask you something, sir?'

'Of course.'

'Well, it's just something that's been bugging me ever since this whole thing began. Why me? Why did I come back into your time? I don't even come from your country, let alone your town.'

There was a pause.

'I know not,' Shakespeare said slowly. He stared at Cal, his eyes searching the boy's face, as if trying to read something in the thin, freckled features. Suddenly he caught his breath. 'But I can guess . . . ' he paused for a

146

moment. 'Yes, I can guess . . . And that makes the grief somewhat easier to bear.'

'Why . . . ?' Cal began but the word was caught up in the evening breeze that stirred the roses in the arbour, releasing a heavy scent into the air. 'Why . . . ?'

Roses and something else, something familiar to this place . . . lavender and thyme and the memory of an elderly Chinese lady walking beside him in the timeless garden . . .

And he was back in the present, staring at the house in Henley Street.

A coach was drawn up outside the guest house when Cal returned and luggage was piled high on the pavement. Carole, who had been watching out for him, hailed him with relief.

'Hi! We were beginning to figure you'd maybe decided to stay behind.'

Cal climbed on to the coach as the group shouted goodbyes, stowed their luggage, and clambered noisily aboard. He took a seat at the back and stared out of the window.

There were few people in the street. A woman with a child. Two other women talking on the corner. A tall, thin man walking quickly towards the coach. He had a lean face and hair just turning grey at the temples. An unremarkable man, the kind who would not stand out in a crowd. The man started to run and Cal suddenly jerked to attention.

In an instant he was off the coach and running, running down the street to meet him.

'Dad! Oh, Dad . . . '

Much later on, Cal sat beside another window, this time looking out into Bridge Street. The coach had long since departed, a disappointed Carole waving frantically from the back. His luggage had been moved to his father's hotel

147

and a room booked. They had walked round the town, hardly speaking, content to be together. And finally they had ended up in McDonald's Restaurant.

'Why did we have to come here?' his father said, struggling back to the table with boxes full of food. 'Couldn't you think of a more traditional meal on my first night in England?'

Cal looked at him without smiling. 'In a way, it all started here,' he said.

'What did?'

Cal considered. 'No, that's not right. Perhaps it really started at the Birthplace.'

'Cal, you've been throwing out dark hints for the last hour and I still don't know what you're talking about.'

Cal gave him a look. 'Okay. But you mightn't believe me.'

He began his story, letting his hamburger and french fries go cold. He started hesitantly, fearing that his father would scoff or dismiss it out of hand, but grew more confident as he listened intently and did not interrupt.

He's never listened to me in this way before, Cal thought suddenly, and I've never talked to him in this way before. We've never really talked at all. He was astonished at the thought and his voice faltered.

'What happened?' his father asked in the pause.

Cal picked up the thread and finished the story. There was a long silence.

'I said you mightn't believe me,' Cal said defensively. 'But it all *did* happen though. Honest.' He bent his head and began slowly eating the cold meal.

'I'd like to meet your Nicky,' his father said at last.

There was another silence.

'I'd like to have met Shakespeare too,' he said, a strange note in his voice. Cal caught the inflection.

'You *don't* believe me, do you,' he said.

'Oh, I do, Cal. I swear I do.'

'You *do?*' Cal asked, almost in disbelief.

His father nodded. He looked pre-occupied and Cal studied him closely.

'No, you don't.' He felt deflated. 'I guess it does all sound pretty crazy.'

'Crazy or not, I believe you.'

Cal sat back in relief. 'Oh, wow— that's just . . . But *why*? I mean . . .'

Calvin Senior smiled. 'Trying to make me change my mind or something? Look, Cal, I believe your story for a number of reasons. First, you're truthful. Second, you couldn't know so much about the period or the people in it. Third, why go to the trouble of making it up? And fourth . . . ' his father paused. There was a certain tension in him, an excitement held in check. Cal caught his mood.

'Yeah?'

'Well, there is, or there may be, corroboration of a kind that you can't possibly know about,' his father said slowly. '*Love's Labour's Won* might never turn up, as your dubious guide so rightly pointed out. There are a number of fabulously rich private collectors in the world who would snap it up just for the pleasure of gloating over it. But there again, who knows?' He paused. 'But very recently a document—or rather a fragment of a document—*has* come to light, and set Shakespearian scholars a great puzzle.'

Cal was silent.

'There is a signature and a date. The signature is reputed to be that of Susanna Shakespeare and the date is the 14th of September 1596.'

Cal stared at him in growing excitement.

'What does it say?'

'I haven't seen it myself, but it's set a fine riddle among the scholars. There's a reference to a manuscript that was taken and something about a stranger . . . '

'That's *me!*' Cal shouted. 'It must be! She must have written about it. She must have written it all down!'

His father grinned at him. 'Hold on and I'll try to remember some more . . . ' He thought for a moment. 'There was something about a woman, and the word "restoration". Then the reference to the stranger . . . "who was no stranger, but of our own kin . . . " Something like that. I'm hoping to see a copy soon—maybe even the original.'

' "Who was no stranger but of our own kin",' Cal repeated. 'What's that mean?'

His father looked surprised. 'I would have thought that obvious.'

'But the stranger's *me*!'

'Well, if the document is genuine—and it's being hotly debated and subject to all sorts of tests at the moment,' his father added cautiously, 'and if the stranger *is* you—and that does seem likely from all you've told me—then the connection is clear.'

'Not to me.'

'Haven't I ever told you?'

'What?'

'I didn't think of it, I suppose. And then it wouldn't have meant anything to you. It's not something one boasts about—well, not something *I'd* boast of anyway. But I suppose it was just one of the many reasons why Shakespeare became rather special to me,' his father said thoughtfully.

'Are you telling me that we're connected to Shakespeare?' Cal asked slowly. '*Related* to him?'

His father smiled. 'Oh, not directly. There are no direct descendants. Susanna had one daughter, Elizabeth, and she had no children. Judith had three children, but they were all childless. No, our connection is through his sister, Joan. She married a man called William—William Hart.'

'I saw him,' Cal said thoughtfully. 'He was at the meal I told you about. Hamnet said he'd marry his aunt that year.'

'Hamnet was a bit premature, for William didn't marry Joan until 1599. But they did marry and did have children—four children. One became an actor and never married, two died young but the fourth, Thomas, married and it's descendants of his that are scattered around, some in this country, some overseas after they emigrated in the last century. As far as we know, they settled in Australia, New Zealand, and the States.'

Cal looked bemused and his father smiled again. 'Think of your *name*, Cal!'

'Calvin Hartfield Junior,' Cal said slowly. '*Hartfield*. William Hart. Of course!'

He sat back in his chair, trying to take it in.

'So you see why I believe you?' his father said after a pause.

'Yeah. Sure.'

'I'm just envious—but glad for you as well.'

'Even though I screwed it up?' Cal asked wryly.

His father was silent for a moment. 'You could say I screwed things up too, couldn't you? Yet here we are, sitting talking to each other in a way we haven't before. We can't all be success stories. If I'd been in your position I expect I'd have done exactly the same, maybe a whole lot worse.'

'You really mean that?'

'Sure.'

The weight of responsibility and guilt that Cal had felt ever since the manuscript had been taken from him seemed to lift gently from his shoulders.

'Cal.' His father stopped. 'Cal—I don't know quite how to say this. I've not been a success story cither. I walked out and left you . . . '

Cal sat very still.

'I can say I'm sorry but that's inadequate, I know. I did try, but I should have tried harder. I watched you a couple of times. I stood outside your school gates and watched you

151

and felt proud. That's my son, I thought. But I always walked away before you came out. I'm good at walking away . . . ' he said bitterly. He stood up abruptly. 'You finished? I need some fresh air after that flight.'

They left the restaurant and turned towards the river. They were both deep in their own thoughts and did not speak, but it was a warm and companionable silence. They walked down Bridge Street without noticing their surroundings and passed a news-stand whose headlines screamed:

STRATFORD ACTOR DIES
IN MOTORWAY INFERNO

but neither of them gave it a glance.

They crossed the bridge and ambled along the path, past gaily coloured boats that were moored for the night, people strolling at their ease in the warm, still air, and fishermen, intent and silent. Eventually they sat down on the grass opposite the weir.

'It was around here Hamnet drowned,' Cal said at last.

'Yes.'

Cal looked at him. 'I like this place,' he said simply. 'It's got a kind of peace . . . '

'Sure.'

'He knew, you know. Shakespeare. About my being a relation. A kinsman. Or he guessed. He must have told Susanna. He said it made Hamnet's death easier to bear.'

'I'm glad.'

They fell silent, looking out across the river.

'Everything's settled, by the way,' his father said at last. 'There'll be no more fighting in the courts.'

'And Mom?'

'She's okay.'

Cal was quiet for a moment.

'And me?'

His father looked at him. 'It'll be up to you to choose.' He looked away. 'I can't expect anything, of course, and I wouldn't want you to make any decision in a hurry. You've got to think of your schooling for a start.' He paused. 'I'll be staying over here for a year or two. I've been appointed to a post as visiting professor at Birmingham University.' He laughed. 'It means a big drop in pay but then I never was bothered too much about that kind of thing.' He paused again. 'I guess I might rent an apartment here, or take a house. It all depends . . . ' He stopped.

Cal glanced at him and was shocked at the mingled look of longing and defeat that was in his father's eyes. He felt a sudden rush of love for him, so strong that his eyes prickled, but he said nothing, just punched him roughly on the shoulder. His father glanced away for a moment.

'So what was it all about, Dad?' Cal asked, wanting to break the tension. 'Why did I go back into the past?'

His father looked at him and smiled. 'Who can say? Perhaps—to put it grandly—as a catalyst for change. Perhaps to befriend Hamnet . . . '

'That's what Shakespeare said,' Cal said thoughtfully.

They sat in silence, watching the evening sun shine golden on the rippled surface of the water, as it had done since time immemorial. Then they stood up and walked slowly back along the river.

'I'll take you to the Birthplace tomorrow, Dad. I'll take you everywhere.'

'Yes,' said his father. 'You do that. I want to see everything. With you.'

Epilogue

' . . .He has gone and I do not expect we shall see him again. But his coming was timely, not only for that which he tried to do in restoring the manuscript. He brought to the light of day things that should never have been hidden—relationships in disharmony and those that were ill-advised. But he did more, and more than he can possibly know. Father told me and I rejoice that the stranger has played some part in healing the terrible grief of my brother's death . . . '

The writing stopped as a fresh gust of wind blew the heavy scents of early autumn in through the open window. Roses . . . lavender . . . thyme . . . Susanna raised her head and looked out into the garden.

A figure had emerged from the old barn, a slight figure with light-brown hair brushed severely back from a protruding forehead. A cloak was wrapped around her dress and trailed behind her as she slowly crossed the grass towards the house.

Shakespeare rose from his seat in the shelter of the arbour and waited for her to reach him. Judith stopped a few paces away and they stood staring at one another. He opened wide his arms and Judith ran into them and was enfolded in an embrace.

Susanna smiled. Then she reached once more for the parchment sheet.

' "Restoration of a kind will happen, one with another". This was told me by the wise woman. Her prophecy proved true. I pray God that the stranger, who was no stranger, but of our own kin, may know such blessings among his own people and in his own time.

154

'As witness to this account and the events that have here befallen, I, Susanna Shakespeare, set my hand and seal, this fourteenth day of September, in the year of our Lord, 1596.'

She signed the document, laid it to one side, then rose and went out into the garden.

Fact and Fiction

In writing *The Shakespeare Connection* I have tried, wherever possible, to base the story on fact. *Love's Labour's Won*, the play central to the plot, did, as far as we know from the sources mentioned in my book, exist, although whether or not by Shakespeare is not known. What is fiction is the loss of the manuscript and all that followed.

Shakespeare married Anne Hathaway in 1582 and six months later Susanna was born. The twins, Hamnet and Judith, were born two years after that. Shakespeare seems to have left Stratford soon after the birth of the twins. By 1592 he was sufficiently well established in the London theatre to be the subject of an envious attack by a rival playwright, Robert Greene, though of his whereabouts in the intervening years nothing is known. As far as we know, his wife and children remained in Stratford, living in the house in Henley Street which is reputedly Shakespeare's birthplace. All the details relating to Shakespeare's family and relations in Stratford are fact, as far as is known or conjectured.

Superstition and belief in witchcraft was widespread in Elizabethan England and neither Shakespeare, nor his children, would have had difficulty in believing Cal's story. The white witch was a commonplace of country life and people were even proud of their local wise woman. 'Goody' Bromley was, in fact, a well-known wise woman of Stratford.

In 1596, the date in which I have set my story, Shakespeare was 32 years old and a successful playwright, actor, and member of 'The Lord Chamberlain's Men' at

The Theatre in Shoreditch, London. On 11 August his only son, Hamnet, was buried. The death is recorded but the cause of death is not known.

Shakespeare's life in London, as a member of 'The Lord Chamberlain's Men' is likewise fact. The company included the following players mentioned in the book— Samuel Gilburne, Henry Cundall, and Richard Burbage—and it is believed that the name of the bookholder (the present-day equivalent would be stage manager) was a man named Thomas Vincent. I have invented the names of the apprentices and other lesser characters. In 1596 'The Lord Chamberlain's Men' were playing principally at The Theatre and at The Cross Keys Inn. They did not move to their more famous theatre, The Globe, until 1599. The company held a pre-eminent position in the Elizabethan theatre and were summoned to Court from time to time to play before the Queen.

John Loveday, Richard Wantage, Philip Sturley, and Anthony Barnard and all the circumstances surrounding the disappearance and reappearance of the manuscript are, of course, pure fiction, as is Susanna's document on the events, although from time to time there are instances where hitherto lost manuscripts, paintings, and other works of art have been found.

Shakespeare died in 1616 at the age of 52, having assured his immortality as the world's greatest playwright in the thirty-seven plays and hundred and fifty-four sonnets he left behind. Susanna married John Hall, an eminent Stratford doctor and died in 1649 at the age of 66. Judith married Thomas Quiney, a man with a rather shady reputation in Stratford, and died at the age of 77.

Descendents of Shakespeare through his sister Joan do exist, both in Great Britain, the United States, New Zealand, and Australia, although none of them, to my knowledge, bear the name Hartfield.

If we shadows have offended,
Think but this, and all is mended,
That you have but slumber'd here
While these visions did appear.
And this weak and idle theme,
No more yielding but a dream.

A Midsummer Night's Dream